EVERYTHING WE MIGHT Have Been

AN EXTRA SERIES ALTERNATE HISTORY NOVEL

EVERYTHING WE MIGHT HAVE BEEN

Cover Design by Melissa Williams Design

Locker and Books by Liudmyla, Adobe Stock

Backpack by ONYXprj, Adobe Stock

Rose by pandavector, Adobe Stock

Lights by andrew_rybalko, Adobe Stock

Janci's author photo by Michelle D. Argyle

Megan's author photo by Heather Cavill

Published by Garden Ninja Books

ExtraSeriesBooks.com

First Edition: September 2019

0 9 8 7 6 5 4 3 2 1

EVERYTHING WE MIGHT HAVE BEEN

AN EXTRA SERIES ALTERNATE HISTORY NOVEL

MEGAN WALKER & JANCI PATTERSON

For Lauren Janes,
who will always be our Barbie girl

ONE

Felix

I'm sitting in health class at ten in the morning, staring at the empty seat two rows ahead of me. That seat is occasionally occupied by Jenna Rollins, when she feels inclined to grace us with her presence. Jenna is a senior in a class full of juniors, but it's not hard to guess why she might need to repeat it.

I wish she'd failed some other junior level class. Some class I'm not in, staring at her pale shoulders and upper back while she sits there in some leather corset and short skirt, with her dyed-black hair twisted up in those crazy buns that make her look like a cross between the devil and Minnie Mouse.

For the thousandth time, I tell myself I shouldn't be attracted to her. My last girlfriend was a flutist in orchestra with me, and she was cute and flirty and all right to talk to in small doses, and pretty much the opposite of Jenna Rollins in every possible way.

But the truth is, sometimes when class gets boring—which is most of the time, because there's only so many ways you can be told not to smoke, drink, do drugs, or have unprotected sex—I think about what Jenna would say if she ever bothered to put two words together in my direction.

It'll never happen. It's a stupid fantasy. But there's not a lot else to do in health class, so it passes the time.

It's the amount of fantasizing I do about her everywhere else that really bothers me.

Up at the front of the room, Ms. Crandall is pulling baby dolls out of a box and lining them up on the table. The plastic babies are mercifully quiet, but I know that's not going to last much longer. It's one of those stupid assignments that's supposed to teach us that having a baby is hard, but is really just going to teach us that being in health class sucks, as does having to care for the needs of a robot baby whose only goal in life is to torment you into practicing safe sex.

In his seat in the front row, my friend Daniel is turning bright red. I can tell from four rows back, even though he's wearing long sleeves and the only part of him I can see is the back of his neck.

Daniel is a Mormon and has sworn himself to Jesus or something, because he's not allowed to have sex until he's married. Daniel is nothing if not an overachiever, so I'm pretty sure he plans to make it to his wedding night without ever having made eye contact with a member of the opposite sex outside of his immediate family. His younger sister Ginnie told me that when he first learned about periods, he wouldn't look *her* in the eye for a month.

I tear a strip of lined paper out of the bottom of my notebook, ball it up, and flick it at the back of Daniel's beet-red neck. Daniel swats at his neck like he expects it was a fly, and then turns around to glare at me.

His face looks like a tomato, and I snicker at him. Daniel rolls his eyes and looks like he wants to flip me off, but won't because Jesus hates middle fingers.

I get this look from Daniel a lot. But he's still going to be my partner for our week of caring for animatronic humans, because no matter how much I mock him, I've still got the highest average in the class. He wants someone who'll do their homework, and I want someone who isn't on a sports team and can therefore take the kid for the four-hour space after school when I practice cello every day. I'll get up in the middle of the night and pat the robot if I have to, but I cannot be interrupting my practice constantly to bounce the thing and feed it fake milk or whatever I'm going to have to do that's supposed to convince me I don't want to have a kid for another decade or so. And I don't think my private cello teacher would appreciate hearing that my fingering exercises are being disturbed for some health class assignment. I may be between competitions, but that doesn't mean I'm allowed to slack off. Not if I want to be ready for Juilliard auditions next year.

I'm glad Daniel and I discussed this beforehand, because Angela Harwick keeps turning in her seat and smiling at me. She's clearly eyeing me for her partner, but she's friends with my ex-girlfriend Julia, who throws enough shade at me already without me fake shacking up with one of her friends from the flute section.

"All right," Ms. Crandall says after she finishes emptying the box. "We have the same number of boys and girls in this class, so the partnerships will all be even."

I stare at her. She's already paired us up? I mean, I have nothing against doing this project with a girl, especially if there was a girl I was interested in who I actually had a chance with, but—

I raise my hand. "Ms. Crandall?"

Ms. Crandall looks up at me. "Yes, Felix."

"Isn't that premise a little discriminatory? After all, gay couples can legally adopt children, or use a surrogate if they want to."

Ms. Crandall gives me a dubious look. "That's true. But this is health class, not an adoption agency, so I think that for our purposes—"

"I thought the purpose of this assignment is to simulate our future child-rearing experiences," I say. "If I'm gay, can I have a guy partner?"

Giggles erupt around the room. Daniel, who Jesus will also not allow to be gay, has put his head down on his desk and died. I feel somewhat self-satisfied with this.

"Are you coming out right here in class, Felix?" Ms. Crandall says.

If it means I can work with a partner who won't be a slack-ass who leaves our robot baby in a car overnight and lowers our grade, I sure as hell will. That's probably offensive in and of itself—me being willing to claim a sexuality that people get persecuted for as a means to maintain my grade point average.

But I'm still going to do it. "If I do, can Daniel be my partner?"

More laughter. Daniel somehow manages to shoot me a death glare without removing his head from the surface of his desk.

"No, Felix," Ms. Crandall says. "What you and Daniel do on your own time is your business, as is your sexual orientation. But as this is merely a simulation of a family experience, you'll work with the partner you're assigned to."

I sigh. Ms. Crandall gives the rest of the details about the assignment—it runs for a week, and we have to check our doll in every day in class, where the computer will tell Ms. Crandall how we're doing. We get docked a tenth of a letter grade for every incident of parental neglect, but if we improve throughout the week, there's a sliding scale. I'm looking around the room at all the stoners and slackers I could get paired with, and suddenly working with Julia's friend Angela doesn't seem like a half-bad idea.

Ms. Crandall starts announcing partners and handing out babies, like health class is some kind of adoption service run by Oprah. Daniel gets assigned to Angela, and she looks longingly back at me while he appears to be trying to retract his head into his body like a turtle.

There go my first and second choices. I'm looking around at the other girls and deciding who I think might be a halfway passable partner when Ms. Crandall reaches my name.

"Felix Mays," Ms. Crandall says. "And Jenna Rollins." She picks up a baby and puts it on my desk, and then continues down her list. I'm staring right at her, but I'm not really seeing.

No.

No, no, no.

She cannot have assigned me to do a homework assignment with *Jenna Rollins*.

Jenna doesn't do homework. She barely comes to class. She doesn't give the time of day to nerds like me, and I actually need someone to do their half of this assignment.

I raise my hand again. "Ms. Crandall?" I ask. "Could I have a partner who's actually in this class?"

Ms. Crandall looks at me. "Jenna Rollins is in this class, Felix," she says in a weary tone. "She sits two desks in front of you."

I know that. I can't *not* know that. Jenna is easily the hottest girl in school—not that she would care that I or anyone else thinks this. She doesn't seem to care what people think in general, and she definitely isn't the type to bother with any of the stupid high school social games—though maybe that shouldn't be a surprise, given that she barely even bothers with high school. Regardless, she's so far out of my league that we might as well be on different planets.

They say Jenna Rollins will sleep with anyone, but it isn't true. Drop-dead-gorgeous, hella-cool senior girls with sexy punk style and college boyfriends don't do high school orchestra nerds. Not even the first chair cello.

Jason Amala leans over in his seat and elbows me. "Dude," he says. "You're totally having a crack baby."

Behind me, someone else snorts. "At least she has enough experience."

That's a good point. "Ms. Crandall," I say again.

She sighs. "Yes, Felix."

"Don't you think you ought to excuse Jenna from this assignment? Because she's obviously got enough experience with—"

"Felix Mays," Ms. Crandall says. "You're going to do this assignment with your assigned partner, or you're going to fail. And this is twenty percent of your quarter grade, do you understand?"

Damn. Yeah, that I understand. "Yes, ma'am."

There's a general chorus of ooooooohs from the class, because

I'm not the kind of student who gets smacked down by the teacher like that. But yeah, okay, it was a little rude of me to bring up that Jenna has a kid.

I stare down at the doll. She's about the size I imagine an infant must be, and surprisingly heavy, though that might be accurate, too, for all I know. Her glassy blue eyes stare back up at me, her mouth permanently pursed in a sucking motion. Her limbs are made out of rubber, and she's distinctly weighted in the behind, where there's a USB port to plug her in for our score.

My child, for the next week, whose mother is Jenna Rollins.

I need to come up with some way to get her to do her half of the work without actually having to spend time around her, or this assignment is going to drive me insane.

I stalk into the cafeteria toward the table where Jenna Rollins sits, carrying the plastic baby by the arm. There's a sensor inside that makes it cry if I drop it—and docks us a tenth of a letter grade, something that seems pretty lenient for the charge of dropping a fake human being—but this sensor doesn't seem to be triggered by my carrying it irresponsibly, and I'm going to take all the freedom from this thing I can get.

Jenna is sitting at her usual table against the back wall, across from a guy in her grade who always wears what I can only describe as a pirate coat. Today he doesn't have a shirt on underneath it, baring his bronze pectorals to the world.

I can only assume he's been buttoning it in class.

Jenna sees me coming and eyes me with disinterest, which is about the only way she ever looks at anyone. She clearly thinks she's too good for high school and homework and us peons who show up to school less than three hours late, and I find myself even more irritated.

Our needy hunk of plastic starts to whine.

I put the baby over my shoulder, give it a few token pats, and when it stops, I step up to Jenna's table and drop it right on top—there goes a tenth of a letter grade. The child is a bit more bouncy than I anticipated, and she rebounds and lands with her nose planted in Jenna's school cafeteria fries.

At least she eats like the plebeians.

"Excuse me," Jenna says, batting her long eyelashes at me with a look of ennui. "What the hell do you think you're doing?"

"I'm dropping your child off for shared custody," I say.

She squints at the doll as if this, too, she's too good for. Her lips purse slightly, and I wish, not for the first time, that she looked like my great aunt Imogen so I didn't have to think about how much I want her.

"It's for health class," I say. "Which you'd know if you'd bothered to show up."

Jenna picks up a plastic fork and uses it to push the baby off of her fries, though it only lands in her ketchup. "And I care *because. . .*"

There it is. The ultimate problem. Jenna isn't any more interested in working with me than she is in dating me, though the former, I suppose, isn't personal.

"I don't know," I say. "Maybe because you're a mother? I mean, you're the one who knows about taking care of babies, right?"

She arches an eyebrow at me.

That was probably low. Everyone knows Jenna Rollins has a kid. She wasn't the only girl at school to get pregnant, but she was the only one to actually give birth in her freshman year.

Still, saying that to her clearly isn't getting her on my side, and I need to actually pass this assignment. If I don't, it'll bring down my entire average.

"I'm not any more thrilled about this than you are," I say. "But I can't take care of it twenty-four-seven. I have practice after school, and I can't stop playing every five minutes to pat the thing."

"Ah," she says. "The cellist can't possibly be disturbed by anything as plebeian as homework."

I blink at her. Apparently she also uses the word plebeian. And knows I'm a cellist, when I honestly hadn't been sure she knew I was breathing before this moment. "Yeah," I say. "Something like that."

"Good luck with that." She gestures at the doll. "And, just a tip, next time you want to pawn your homework off on someone, try *not* tossing it on their french fries first."

I close my eyes for a second and draw a deep breath. I'd known she was going to say that—if not the part about the fries, exactly—so I'm prepared. "Look. I know you don't care about your grade, but we get the same score, no matter who does the work, and I need you to do your half. So I'll pay you."

She pauses, though her vaguely bored expression doesn't change. I wonder if it ever does. "How much?"

"Thirty dollars a day."

Jenna scoffs, and even her pirate friend looks dubious. "I do know how much your father makes, you know."

I doubt she does, but she apparently knows I come from the rich side of the school boundaries. Which is okay. I can afford more than that. "Fifty."

"Two hundred," Jenna says.

"Per *day*? My dad is rich. I'm *not*."

She lifts a french fry and stirs it in the edge of her occupied ketchup. "Then I guess you'll be taking care of your poor motherless baby all by yourself."

Ugh. Fine.

"One hundred a day. Final offer."

Jenna looks up at me. Her eyes are a stormy gray, and for the first time she looks interested. "Fine. I'll take it."

"But you actually have to take care of the thing," I say. "It has a sensor inside. Mrs. Crandall is going to hook it up to the computer every day and if we don't get at least a ninety percent—"

"*Ninety?*" Jenna says.

"Ninety percent," I repeat. "If we don't get an A, you don't get paid. I'll pay you daily, after class, as long as the score is right."

She points her spork at the kid. "How do you think we're doing right now, with our child drowning in ketchup? What kind of father are you anyway?"

I roll my eyes. "What kind of mother are *you?*"

Her eyes turn cold again, like I've hit a nerve, and I feel a stab of guilt. I pick up the baby and steal her napkin to wipe off the ketchup. Then I hand the baby to her. "Twelve hours," I say. "I'll take nights and mornings, you take afternoons and evenings. We'll swap before school every day."

"Ten o'clock," Jenna says. "I'm not showing up before then."

Of course she isn't. "Ten o'clock. You'll have to give me your address so I can pick up the kid every night."

Jenna gives me a sarcastic smile and pulls a purple pen out of the backpack slumped next to her. She reaches out and takes my hand and starts to write her address down on the back of it. My arm is tingling where she touches me, and it's all I can do not to lean into her, but I force myself to stay steady.

She's Jenna Rollins, and she's clearly mocking me. She looks up at me and bats her eyelashes. "There are easier ways to get my address. You could have just *asked.*"

"Yeah, no thanks. I'll pass on the syphilis."

"Really?" Jenna says. "And I thought that's what you were here for."

I roll my eyes again. "Don't flatter yourself," I say, and I stalk off across the cafeteria again, at once dreading and looking forward to a few hours from now, when I'll have to talk to her again. Maybe we should have set up some neutral custody switching location, like a McDonalds, like a real divorced couple.

Or maybe I just need to get over the idea that Jenna Rollins would ever look at me as anything other than an annoyance.

TWO

Jenna

The doorbell rings and I look at my phone—10:00. Of course Felix Mays would be punctual down to the minute, even when it comes to starting his shift on plastic baby watch. It could be because he doesn't trust me with the thing one minute longer than necessary, but really I'm guessing it's because his brain will explode if his perfectly structured day is off by sixty seconds.

Not that I mind; I've got plans tonight and they don't include some ridiculous health assignment that hopes to scare kids away from unprotected sex—which, hey, if it works, great. If there's some girl out there that thinks "damn, I want this guy and he wants me but we don't have a condom and I really don't want some freak-ass robot baby that grades me on a daily basis," then more power to her.

I doubt it would've worked for me. I learned that lesson the hard way.

I hear Felix's voice, and my sister Rachel's, from downstairs. He's probably complaining about being partnered with me; she's undoubtedly expressing her sympathy. Really, I bet she's wishing she could be the one playing house with Felix Mays. Maybe he's wishing the same.

I frown and tighten the laces on my Chucks, so I'll be ready to go as soon as he takes his kid.

Then I hear a smaller voice: Ty. My three-year-old son. He says something and Felix laughs, and I get a weird nervous sensation in my chest.

Why did I give him my address? Why didn't I just meet him somewhere? I don't invite guys over to my house, not ever. Or anyone from school in general. I get enough shit from people at school about having a kid, the last thing I want is to expose Ty to any of that. People can say whatever they want about me, but if they bring Ty into it, like Ty specifically because they've *met* him—HELL. NO.

Rachel doesn't have people over either, though I think her reason is because she's afraid I'll be home and scare away her friends. And she barely even talks to *guys*.

I hear footsteps on the stairs and then there's a sharp, impatient knock.

"Come in," I say. "Unless you're afraid you'll catch me naked."

Felix calls my bluff—or maybe he really doesn't care—and walks right in. His face is slightly less glowery than before, but he's still clearly irritated just to be in my presence. Which, whatever. Not that I ever did anything to him.

Probably that's what he's all pissy about.

"Is the kid still alive?" he asks. Felix doesn't seem to be big on preamble.

"See for yourself," I say, gesturing vaguely in the direction of the armchair where our kid is sleeping. Let him think I've barely paid any attention to the thing all day. It's what he's bound to think anyway.

He picks up the baby, and eyes it dubiously. "Ninety percent, remember. If you want the money."

"God, I remember, okay?" I glare at him, and go to my dresser to check my makeup in the mirror. I swipe on some raspberry lip stain, and catch him watching, which sends a little thrill through me. He sees me catch him and looks quickly

15

away. I roll my eyes and turn back around. "You could stand to chill out a bit, you know. Unbunch those panties a little. Maybe loosen that collar?"

I eye his button-up shirt as I say this—which is buttoned all the way up to his neck, even though he's not wearing a tie with it. It's a slim-fitting blue shirt that matches his eyes, and it's not like it looks bad on him. He's actually really hot, and with a smile that, okay, might have caught my eye a time or two, and might have led to some hardcore fantasizing right there in school. Not that he's actually ever smiled at *me*, or is likely to.

Which is too bad for him. My imagination is *good*.

"Chill out?" He raises an eyebrow. "Thanks for the super helpful advice. Have you thought about going into life-coaching?"

I sit down on the bed and watch him try to avoid looking down at my cleavage, which is being displayed nicely by my little black corset top. "Well, I would," I say, crossing my legs casually, "but I'm so busy getting my syphilis treatments."

He has the decency to look abashed, at least. Lots of people wouldn't. He looks down at the baby and clears his throat. "Nice outfit," he says, plucking at the fabric of the footed pajamas I put on it earlier. It has little airplanes on it. Somewhere, my mom has a box of Ty's baby clothes stored away, but I was too embarrassed to ask for that. But this is the one outfit I keep, tucked away in my drawer. It was what he was wearing the first time I heard Ty laugh.

It doesn't sound like Felix is being sarcastic, but I feel instantly wary anyway.

"Yeah, we have some baby clothes lying around," I say with a shrug. "I know it's boy clothes and I'm pretty sure she's a girl, but whatever."

"Girls can like planes," he says. "Maybe she'll be a pilot."

"I don't know. I've heard the Air Force is pretty discriminatory against androids."

His lips twitch at an almost-smile, and he looks a little surprised. Like it's some big shock that the school slut might

16

actually have a sense of humor. My gut twists, and I pick at the purple polish on my nails.

"Your kid is cute," he says, and I look back up, and now I'm the one looking surprised. "I met him downstairs," he says, using the baby doll to gesture awkwardly at the stairs. "He told me about the Christmas Tree of Doom. That's . . . that's pretty cool."

I snort. "Rachel doesn't think so." But I can't help but grin. I get a little too much amusement out of the whole thing, admittedly. Both out of Ty pretending to be a knight who has to fight the evil Christmas tree, and out of Rachel miserably going along with the game, knowing she's going to be stuck cleaning up all the ornaments—or Orbs of Evil—that he takes down every night. It's May and the tree is still up, because Ty cries whenever my parents talk about taking it down.

Rachel might have good reason to think of me as a major pain in the ass.

"Yeah, well, Ty seems to like it," Felix says.

Something catches in my throat at hearing him say Ty's name, and I shift uncomfortably. "Seems like he does," I say. Not that I really know much of what Ty likes, as Rachel often reminds me. Whatever. From our earlier conversation, it's clear Felix already knows I'm a shitty mom. No point trying to pretend otherwise. I shrug. "I'm not really around enough to know."

There's this pause, this heavy moment of silence, and for some reason it reminds me of the afternoons I sit outside the music room and listen to him play the cello. I started doing that late last year, after my parents had to sell our piano to get a little extra cash. I wanted to play the school's piano, but definitely didn't want anyone to hear me play or sing. But I'd soon discovered that Felix uses the music room every day, playing his cello for hours. At first I was super annoyed, having to sit outside against the lockers, drawing on my sneakers—and okay, maybe a few lockers—with Sharpies to keep myself occupied until he left.

But it didn't take long before I started just listening, rapt.

Listening to the rock and Johnny Cash covers. Listening to the fast-paced pieces that make my fingers drum against the linoleum. Listening to the slow, somber pieces that wring out my heart. Listening intensely even to the silences between pieces, which echo with the weight of the previous final note and somehow also with the heady anticipation of the next opening one.

I'm not usually one for classical music, or Johnny Cash for that matter, but Felix Mays can play a damn cello.

Not that it matters, really. Not that musical talent or even a great smile means a guy isn't an entitled, uptight jerk who clearly thinks he's too good for someone like me.

Except Rachel says he's a good guy, and she's actually pretty accurate on these things. And he may be rich, but he works his ass off on the cello, so it's not like he expects to make it on his parent's money and his good looks.

So maybe he's just uptight.

And maybe he *is* too good for someone like me.

There's a dull ache in my chest, which is a feeling I hate. And a feeling I know how to get rid of, for the night anyway.

"So you have the kid. Is there anything else you're going to offer to pay me for?" I ask, narrowing my eyes. His cheeks go a little pink, and his lips tighten. "Because if not, you know, some of us actually have plans tonight."

"Oh yeah?" He folds his arms across his chest. "You have big plans, huh? On a Monday night."

"There's a party." If there's one thing I've learned living in Los Angeles, it's that there's always a party somewhere.

He glowers down at our fake baby, and I'm not sure what prompts me, but I find myself blurting out, "You could come with. You know, if you want."

He looks at me skeptically.

"Right," I say with a forced laugh. "Parties aren't your thing. You might get wasted and end up with an eighty-five percent on something."

"I go to parties," he says defensively. "I don't get wasted. But I go."

18

"So is that a yes?" I don't like how much I'm hoping it is. And I sure as hell hope he can't tell.

"Yeah, sure. I'll go."

Even though I'm weirdly hoping for it, his response catches me off-guard. "Really?"

"Yeah. I told you I go to parties." He tilts his head to the side a bit. "Or were you just asking because you thought I'd say no?"

"No, I—" I toy with one of the cheap silver rings on my finger. "Okay, then. We'll go." I look him over again, which is not an unpleasant activity. "But you can't go like that."

"Like what? A normal person? Wearing normal person clothes?" But he doesn't look offended. If anything, he's got that almost-smile back. I wonder if I could ever get a real smile out of him.

It makes me think of when I see him sitting at his cafeteria table with his orchestra friends and the other assorted preppy crew he hangs out with. How he flirts with the girls, and they eat it up, and I inevitably wonder what it would be like to be one of them. To be the kind of girl a guy like him looks at like that.

Though then I remember it might mean I'd be as annoying as his ex-girlfriend Julia, and I'd probably kill myself after a day of listening to myself talk.

"They aren't exactly college party clothes," I say.

He shifts uncomfortably. "Well, unless you have something else here—"

"I actually do."

He eyes my piles of dirty clothes—which are scattered around my room like little black mountains—with some amount of trepidation. Which, yeah. That's fair. But it's not like I'm planning on dressing him in corsets or lacy bras.

I dig through a pile by my closet, looking for a guy's black leather jacket I have. I don't know whose it is, but I woke up one morning in a frat house game room, and it was the only thing I was wearing, draped on me like a blanket. There was no one there with me, and I couldn't find my shirt, so I took it. I figure its owner probably got a good time off me, and I got a new jacket out of it, so we're both happy.

Except I can't bring myself to wear it again, and didn't even want to look at it until now.

"Here." I hand him the jacket.

He eyes it for a minute, and then puts it on. And damn, it looks good on him. Enough to make me forget where it came from.

"And . . . here," I say, and step up close enough to him to unbutton just that top button. He smells good, fresh and soapy, not doused in Axe Body Spray like most of our classmates, and I can feel my pulse beating in my ears. My fingers linger on the button a moment longer than necessary, and then I step away. "That's better."

"Yeah?" He sounds a little out of breath.

"Yeah," I say, and find myself suddenly self-conscious. Which is weird. I *like* getting that reaction from guys. I tug at the hem of my short skirt.

He clears his throat. "So what are we going to do about our baby?"

"Rachel can watch it," I say. And judge me for abandoning another child. She'll enjoy that.

He frowns. "We shouldn't just dump it on her."

"Don't worry, I'll pay her." It occurs to me that Rachel won't be so upset about watching my fake baby as she will about me taking Felix to a party. She'll assume I'm doing this just to spite her. That I'll sleep with him just because she likes him—though it's not like I go around purposely poaching guys from her or anyone else just for kicks.

She doesn't know about me sitting outside the music room nearly every afternoon. She doesn't know about how my heart beats faster when he comes out, carrying his cello case.

She doesn't need to know. Let her think what she wants. I'll take Felix to this party and I'll sleep with him, and I'll know that he's no different from all the other guys. That he can call me a slut in one breath and with the next not be able to say anything at all because he's too busy fucking me. Just so he can go back to school and his perfect life and brag to his perfect friends about slumming it with me.

And maybe then I can finally get over him.

"Let's go," I say, and force a smile as I lead him downstairs.

I pawn the baby off on Rachel—enduring her judgmental look and trying not to notice the real hurt behind it—and climb into Felix's car. It's a nice Toyota—not as flashy as the mustang convertibles and fully-loaded Lexuses that lots of the other rich kids drive. I find I like this better. It's less pretentious.

"So," he says as we buckle up. "Where's this party?"

"In the Valley." I've got the address on my phone, but I can worry about that as we get closer.

His hands tighten on the steering wheel and he lets out an irritated-sounding little huff. "Did you really want me to come to the party with you? Or did you just want a ride? Because if you do, you could just ask. I'll take you."

Something about that—maybe the way he says it, I don't know—makes that dull achy feeling in my chest less dull. Which is weird. He's said a lot worse things to me today, in a lot pissier of a tone, but this gets me.

Maybe some of that other stuff did too.

"Fine, yeah. Whatever," I say. If he thinks I would just invite him so I could get a ride, fine. Maybe I will.

I'm Jenna Rollins. I'm a straight-up bitch who uses people.

I stare out the window as we drive toward the freeway. Neither of us says anything for several minutes.

And then he does. "So, you go to parties in the Valley a lot?"

He doesn't sound super judgmental about it, but I can't help but think that he is. Valley parties would be hardcore slumming for a guy like him.

"Yeah. So?"

He pauses. "Do you really want to go to the party? Because if you want to, we could go somewhere else."

21

And there it is. He doesn't even want to drive me to the party before he gets his jollies off.

Not that I don't want to have sex with him; he's hot, after all, and my plan to see that he's no different from the other guys is well-intact and chugging along quicker than I thought.

But somewhere, deep down, I'd stupidly hoped he would be different. Even after what an ass he was to me in the cafeteria. I'd stupidly thought maybe some of what I'd felt listening to his music was a part of him. And that part of him might actually—what? Somehow see me differently than the others do? See there's something else there at all?

Stupid stupid stupid.

I learned a long time ago not to believe that anyone is ever going to want more from me than my body. And I learned a long time ago not to care.

THREE

Felix

'm kicking myself for asking Jenna if she wants to go somewhere with me. She's shooting me a look that says this suggestion is wearying, and I get it. Sure, my body is still buzzing from the way her hands felt against my collar, her fingers brushing ever so gently down the side of my lapel. Even through the shirt, they'd felt like fire and longing and I want this girl way more than I have any right to, given that I'm driving to a party where within twenty minutes she's going to have ditched me.

I think that's why I said that. Because even though I know this is going nowhere, I can't help but cling on, practically begging her not to reject me. Even though I know the last thing Jenna Rollins wants is to ditch her friends and her life to hang out with me.

Unlike me, she actually *has* a life.

"Yeah, okay," she says. "Where did you have in mind?"

My mind sputters. Um, nowhere. Because I never in a million years thought that this girl—this gorgeous, *sexy*, way-too-cool-for-me girl—would say *yes* to an invitation like that.

From me. Jenna Rollins wants to spend time with *me*.

"I don't know," I say. "We could like, hang out." I cringe. Yes, Felix. Very smooth. Way to make her instantly regret accepting your offer.

Jenna shakes her head, but she does turn back toward me. "If you want to have sex you can just say so. You could pull over right here if you want."

A stuttering sound comes out of my mouth that sounds like I'm having a stroke.

Jenna gives me a sly look. "What? I'm just saying, you don't have to beat around the bush. I have a reputation for a reason."

I take a deep breath and try to regain my powers of speech. It's not that I don't want to. God, do I want to. I've got a hard-on just thinking about it.

"And what then?" I say, when I can finally string two words together.

"Um, then I blow your mind, and you drive me back home, and tomorrow you can tell everyone you banged me?" she says. "Or not. It's up to you."

I shake my head. "I don't want that."

She looks hurt, and I shake my head again. "No, I don't mean I don't want *you*, I just—" I sigh. This is coming out all wrong. "That's just not how I want this to go."

"Okaaaaaaay," Jenna says. "You tell me how it should go."

My mind is reeling, trying to catch up to my mouth. What do I want? With *her*? "I'll take you out," I say. "Our options are limited this time of night, so probably we'll just go through the Wendy's drive-thru and get Frosties and then go hang out somewhere. Like that dirt lot where you can see the Hollywood sign."

I glance over at her, but she just looks confused. "So you want to have sex in the dirt lot."

"*No!*" I say. "I'm sorry. I clearly suck at explaining this. I'm not really a sex on the first date kind of guy, you know? I've never done that before."

Oh god. I did not just say that. "I mean, I've had *sex* before. Just not the first time I go out with a girl. Only with, like, my girlfriend. It's not something I want to—" I trail off, because I sound like a complete idiot.

"Really?" Jenna says. "Because if I have a Frosty, my mouth will be all cold, and I can do all *kinds* of wonderful things with my tongue. . ."

A shiver runs through me, and I can tell Jenna notices. I force myself to continue, to not imagine her tongue on—oh god. No. No. I can't treat her like that. I don't want to. "And I'd definitely kiss you. And probably we'd make out. Like, second base." I wince. I sound like I'm in seventh grade. "God, this must seem so childish to you."

She gives me a look. "And what exactly does second base mean to you?"

"Ummm," I say. "There's only one second base. It means the same thing to me as everybody."

She shakes a finger at me. "No, tell me what it means."

I sigh. "Fine. So first base is kissing, and second is touching above the waist. Nothing below. Right?"

She shrugs.

"Seriously?" I say. "You have some other definition of second base?"

"I'd include everything with hands in second base. So, like, I could give you a hand job."

I let out an involuntary groan and Jenna smirks at me. Oh, yes. She knows exactly what she's doing to me.

"No," I say. "Thanks."

"Yeah," she says. "Wouldn't want to catch syphilis."

My throat closes. Oh, god, those things I said. "I'm sorry. I should never have said that to you. It was out of line."

She shrugs and hunches in her seat. "It was pretty douchey, yeah."

The soft way she says it—it's different from any tone I've heard her take before. It takes me a minute to speak past the lump in my throat.

"I hurt you," I say.

She shrugs again, but it's clear I'm right. "Yeah, well," she says. "I'd liked you for a while."

25

My head spins at the idea that Jenna Rollins could like me. *Me.* Yeah, sure, I don't exactly have problems getting girls, but she's used to so much more than I'd ever be able to give her. "I'd liked you for a while, too," I say.

She shakes her head. "Oh, *really*."

"I did. But I knew you were out of my league, you know? Like, I knew I didn't have a chance with you."

She looks up, surprised. "What?"

"I mean, you date college guys, right? Not orchestra nerds."

"I don't *date* college guys," she says. "I'm not the kind of girl guys *date*."

I look over at her. "Like, never?"

She squirms.

"Oh, god," I say. "You've *never* been on a date?"

"Not until now. If that's what this is turning into."

It damn well better be, then. And for the first time, I have this glimmer, this image of something I can give her. Something that maybe, if she liked it enough, could turn into something more.

My heart is pounding in my throat. "Yeah, okay. It's a date." I reach out and run a hand over the back of hers as I get off the freeway and flip around to head toward a Wendy's. "Now I'm nervous. I've never dated anyone as beautiful as you."

She gives me another surprised look, and I roll my eyes. "Come on," I say. "You know you're gorgeous."

"I know I'm fuckable. Is that what you meant?"

My mouth falls open. "No, god, that's not—"

"Yeah," Jenna says, softly this time. "I didn't think it was."

I take her hand, and she lets me hold it.

"Are you sure you don't want to just go somewhere and have sex?" she asks.

I smile. "It's not that I don't want to. But what then? We just pretend it didn't happen? Or I'm supposed to brag about it to people? That's not what I want."

"Spell it out for me," Jenna says. "What do you want?"

26

My body is hating me for turning her down, but my heart is humming, and I'm scared to tell her the truth. But she's been treated so badly—god, even I was a total dick to her today—and as sure as I am that she's going to laugh at me and break my heart, I also want to be honest with her. I want to give her that. And maybe when she inevitably shatters me—somehow I already know that's how this is going to end, with my heart torn to shreds—maybe she'll still remember me. Maybe she'll look back and remember there was a guy who treated her decently.

It scares me how badly I want this. "I want you to be my girlfriend. And I want to take you to prom."

"*Prom*," Jenna says. "You want to take me to prom?"

"You've never been, right? I want to get dressed up and pick you up and take you to the dance."

"And *not* have sex."

"Ha, yeah, I don't think I'd hold out very long on that. If you were my girlfriend."

This also terrifies me. I mean, yeah, I had sex with Julia. Kind of a lot, for the five weeks we lasted after we starting sleeping together. But it wasn't great, not like people said it would be. And even though I thought I was in love with her the first time, it became pretty clear to me afterward that I wasn't.

Someone like Jenna, though . . . she's got to be used to guys with all kinds of skills I don't have. Guys who really know what they're doing, who know how to make it into this be-all end-all experience that I don't have the first clue how to create.

Jenna stares at me. "Did you lose some kind of bet? Is this like the plot from *Carrie*?"

"God, no," I say. "I'm really into you. I'm sorry I was a jerk to you before. I think I was just bitter that I'd never have a chance with someone like you. Not that that's an excuse," I add quickly, because I know it's not. I was an asshole, and I shouldn't have been, no matter whether she'd ever notice me or not. "Tell me the truth. Do I have any chance here?"

She's quiet for an agonizingly long moment, and my body is

giving me a long, achy speech about what an idiot I am.

"Yeah," she says finally. "You do. And for the record, I don't think you're an orchestra nerd. I like the way you play."

I leave aside the argument that I am absolutely an orchestra nerd. "You've heard me play?"

She's quiet for a minute. "Yeah. I like to use the piano in the music room, but I don't play in front of people. So I wait for everyone to leave, and sometimes it takes you a *really* long time."

I smile. "You've been listening to me." I love this idea, that she's been hearing me practice after everyone else has left. Even though I didn't know about it, it feels . . . intimate. Far more so than having sex by the side of the road. "You could have told me you needed the room. Or come in and played with me."

"Ah, yes. But this would have required me to tell you that I play. Which I don't. Tell people, that is."

"You play piano. That's awesome." Unwise as it is, it gives me hope that we have something in common. I'm struck with this desire to hear her play, even though she just said she doesn't play in front of people. "What do you like to play?"

She shrugs. "Not classical."

I smile. "Not everything I play is classical."

Jenna looks down at our hands. "Not Johnny Cash, either."

My breath catches. She really has been listening to me play. Enough to be familiar with my music. Or my fondness for Johnny, anyway. "What, then?"

She shrugs again. "A lot of modern indie stuff, some mainstream. Musicals. Maybe some of my own stuff."

"You write your own music?"

She rolls her eyes, like I shouldn't be impressed with this, but I am. I mean, I've done a lot of arranging, especially with the rock stuff, but I'm not a composer. "Yeah," she says. "It's mostly simple stuff. A girl and her piano, you know? Like Sarah Bareilles or Ben Folds, that kind of thing."

"You sing?"

Her silence is an admission in itself.

"You sing, too. And you don't tell anyone."

"Right," Jenna says. "Like, ever."

"So you play and write and sing your own music, but you don't perform?"

"Um, no. Not for years. Not since I was in lessons and had to do recitals."

This is unthinkable to me. The whole point of music, all the long hours of practicing and perfecting, the incredible amount of time it takes to play excellently—the whole purpose is to perform, to share with others this thing that's become part of you. "Will you play for me?" I ask.

Jenna is quiet. "I'm not a real musician. Not like you."

I'd like to be my own judge of that, because I've found that how well people say they can play doesn't usually match up to their actual skill, positive or negative. But I can't imagine Jenna Rollins would go to so much effort to play and not be good at it. "But you don't tell people you play, and you just told me. So I'm hoping maybe I'll be an exception."

"Maybe," she says softly. "You seem to be an exception to many things."

I squeeze her hand. It feels so good, just touching her like that. Even more so being the person she tells things to, and someone she might be willing to play for. Even, I secretly hope, someone she might consider playing music *with*.

"You're sure you don't want to go have sex," she says.

I laugh. "You keep asking me that. I think I already told you I want to. But I'm not going to. Is that a problem for you?"

"I'm still deciding," Jenna says. "I mean, *I* want to have sex with you."

My smile is widening even as my resolve is thinning. I don't want a one-night stand with her, especially not one as callous as a quickie by the side of the road. But if this is more . . . "Okay, here's the deal. You have two options. I'll get us a hotel room, and we can have sex tonight, but only if you want to be my girlfriend. Like publicly. Like, tomorrow at school, everyone can know we're together."

"You don't want to do that," Jenna says. And while I'm not sure which part she's talking about, I know she's wrong.

"I do," I say. "And I also want option two, which is that we'll go to Wendy's and get Frosties and go park and make out and I'm definitely going to ask you for a second date. Your call."

She's quiet, and she doesn't point out that I already did ask her for a second date—to prom—and I don't bring it up either. If I have my way, I'm not waiting that long to take her out again.

I'd take her out every night if she'd let me.

"Let's get the Frosties," Jenna says.

And I smile. "Okay," I say. "Okay."

I focus on not running us off the road—though a few images do fly through my mind of us curled up in the wreckage of my car, kissing through the post-accident adrenaline—until we've been through the drive-thru and made it out to the lot. There are a couple other cars here, but I park in the shadow of a tree near one of the edges. I clear my throat and want to say something, but before I can, Jenna is in my seat with me, her hands on my shoulders and her knees on either side of my thighs. I look up at her, into her eyes, which are just as gray and stormy as ever.

"This is really happening," I say, more to convince myself than anything.

And then her mouth is on mine. She kisses me hard at first, aggressively, and I'm drenched in a full-body rush. There's a lock of dark hair that's fallen from one of her buns, and I push it behind her ear, and run my fingers gently over her cheek. "Jenna," I say, and I look into her eyes, and god I've never felt so much like I'm falling. I kiss her again, softly this time, and she responds back in kind, and for a moment it's like we're suspended in midair, she and I, floating together. Her hand runs up my chest and the shivers are back and I want her, god I want her.

But more than anything, I want her to still want me like

this tomorrow and I'm scared—so scared—of what will happen when I find out I'm just another notch in her bedpost. So I run my hands through her hair and I whisper her name. Jenna takes a sip of her Frosty and runs her cold mouth along my jaw. I gasp and lean my seat all the way back and then she's on top of me and we're rubbing together, both fully clothed and dutifully keeping our hands out of forbidden places, but I know she can feel how turned on I am, how much I want her.

I want her.

She takes another sip and runs her cold tongue along my neck and then my hands are sliding up the backs of her thighs which is technically below the waist, but I stop short of slipping them up her skirt. And I can't help but think of all the things I'd like to do with her, all the ways I'd like to be with her. I want to make love to her, yes, but I also want to hear her play, to play with her, to lie on my bed after school and pretend to do homework and kiss and laugh and take care of our plastic child.

I pull her face back to mine and kiss her again and again, unhooking her corset from her back and running my hands over her chest. She moans softly, like she likes it, and the sound lights me up like a thousand-watt bulb. She unbuttons my shirt, kissing her way down with a cold tongue. She kneels on the floor of my car, her mouth pressing against my stomach, just inches away, and for a moment I'm sure she's going to unbutton my jeans and god I'm going to let her I can't help but let her.

But instead she looks up at me, and crawls back into my lap, and lays her head on my shoulder. We both lie there for a moment, holding each other, breathing.

"Thank you," I say.

She buries her face in my neck, and I can barely make out the words. "Thank you," she says in return.

And I don't know if she means it like I mean it—not just for stopping, for respecting my wishes, but for being here, for wanting me, for giving me a chance to offer her something different than what she's used to, something I'm afraid in the end she won't actually want.

I trail my fingers up and down her arm, and feel goosebumps rising on her skin. I've been with other girls, but I've never felt anything like this, not even close.

And damn if I don't want it to last forever.

FOUR

Jenna

I get back home around two, my head spinning, but not in the same alcohol or pill-fueled way it usually is when I've gone out for the night. I'm buzzed on the memory of my name on Felix's lips, the warmth of his skin under my hands. The way he looked at me, smiled at me, laughed and actually talked with me—between bouts of not being able to keep our mouths off each other, of course. The brush of his fingers against my face as he pushed a lock of hair behind my ear, then as he trailed them down my cheek. I could feel the callouses from his years of cello playing, and his touch set my whole body on fire.

And that moment when I was kneeling between his legs, my lips against the soft skin of his stomach. I could feel how much he wanted me and I wanted him. He didn't seem inclined to stop me, and I almost broke his second base rule before I stopped myself. Because I like him, and I want to be the kind of girl that he respects—god, is that even possible for someone like me? But if so, it has to start with me respecting *him*. I've never been thanked before for *not* going down on a guy. But I'm glad I didn't. Because now I'm alight with this hope that maybe this could be different, a hope that for now, at least, is drowning out my fears. And I mess so many things up, but god,

I don't want to mess this up.

I can't keep from smiling now myself, as I close and lock the door behind me and quietly creep up the stairs to keep from waking anyone up. Not that I have a curfew, or would follow one if I did, but I don't want to deal with my family at the best of times, let alone when I'm coming back from some party.

Or a date.

Did I really just a have a *date* with Felix Mays?

I bite my lower lip to keep from actually giggling at the thought, because seriously, if one mere make-out session—even the best one I've ever had—turns me into one of his bouncy, hair-tossing orchestra fan girls, I'm going to swear off guys forever.

Which would be a real shame, especially now that I've apparently—somehow—got a date to the *prom*. I hope with everything in me that this will still be real tomorrow.

I open the door to my room, and my giddy smile vanishes. Rachel is sitting on my bed, a thick paperback in her hands. Possibly something she's reading for her junior level English class—the class she's in with Felix, even though she's a sophomore, because she's crazy smart—or maybe something she's just reading for fun. Either way, it's undoubtedly some huge classic full of pages-long description of the English countryside and characters engaging in mannered banter over tea.

Her idea of fun and mine are not the same.

She hastily sets the book down when I enter and folds her arms across her chest, glaring at me.

"What the hell are you doing in my room?" I ask, glaring back. Then I see the doll on my chair, wrapped up in a blanket. Still wearing Ty's tiny outfit.

Shit, I was supposed to give it back to Felix for the night. But we both got a little . . . distracted.

"Close the door. You're going to wake Ty up," Rachel says, but jumps off the bed and closes the door herself, like she can't even trust me to be *that* responsible.

"I can't pay you yet for watching the robot," I say, "If that's

34

what you're—"

"What are you doing with Felix Mays?"

Well, that didn't take long.

I roll my eyes and start pulling the pins out of my hair. "Really? Did Mom and Dad not give you the talk?" I wince with one particularly tangled pin. "Don't worry, you didn't miss much. They think the word 'oral' should only apply to dental care."

I turn away as I talk because, for all the lying I've done to my family over the years, my sister has always been better than my parents at seeing through my bullshit. Not *great*, but better.

And I don't know what exactly I *am* doing with Felix, but I can't bring myself to let Rachel or anyone else know that right now.

"So, what, you're just going to use him like you do everyone else?" Rachel says.

I turn back as I free the last pin in my left bun, letting the hair fall down over my shoulder. Rachel's giving me what I think of as the Stinkeye of Judgment, her eyes narrowed, and brows drawn sharply together.

Honestly, it's when she looks like this that I think people are right about how similar she and I look. Aside, of course, from her hair still being our natural dark brown and mine dyed Glam Grunge-black, and her resistance to showing off that she actually has a body somewhere under those loose jeans and too-big polo shirts.

I hate that after all this time her blanket assumptions of me still sting—no matter that they're usually right.

I force a smirk at her. "I guess if that's what I do to everyone, then you have your answer."

"He's a good guy, Jenna. He's talented and smart, and he's actually going somewhere with his life."

Unlike me, on all counts. There's an empty ache in my chest where less than twenty minutes ago, there was a heady mix of heat and chills and something I hadn't felt in so, so long—hope.

She's right, isn't she? Felix couldn't really want me, not in the ways I desperately want him to. He might think he does, might think he sees something more in me.

But what will happen when he sees that he's wrong? That I really am just Jenna Rollins, selfish, fucked-up party girl? What will happen when he decides, wisely, that he's over whatever insanity possessed him tonight to want me as his girlfriend?

He'll go on with his perfect, structured life, and now I won't even be able to go back to sitting outside the orchestra room after school and listening to him play.

The thought hurts more than it has any right to, and that hurt turns me extra bitchy.

"Since you're so obviously into him, were you ever planning on actually *doing* something about it?"

Rachel looks to the side, her cheeks flushing bright pink. She's never had the courage to act on any of her crushes, and we both know it.

"Exactly," I say. "So don't blame me because you refuse to grow a pair and say two words to a cute guy."

"That's not what this is about."

"Isn't it? You aren't just mad because you wish *you'd* spent the night with Felix Mays?" I snap. I know I'm being cruel, but I can't seem to stop. "You wish it was *you* he had his hands all over?"

She flinches, staring down at her fuzzy pug slippers, and I hate myself. She's my sister—my *little* sister, for all that she's the one my parents can count on, the one who takes care of my son more than I ever have. She may not have known how much I liked Felix, but I knew she did.

She deserves better than me. They all do.

I clear my throat, which suddenly feels too tight. "Thanks for watching the doll. I'll get you the money tomorrow."

She shrugs. "Whatever. It's a lot easier than a real baby." She turns to leave and then pauses with her hand on the doorknob. "Just—just don't mess things up for him, okay? He's not like the other guys you screw around with."

I don't say anything in response, and she leaves and goes back into her room, closing her door harder than necessary.

I stand there, numb, and it's a minute or two before I notice that across the hallway, Ty's door is cracked open, his favorite blue stuffed woolly elephant (or is it supposed to be a mammoth?) lying on the floor with its legs poking out around the door jam. I walk over and pick it up, feeling the patches of worn, matted fur that come from being toted around and slept on every day by a toddler.

Did he forget it before bed? Or does he not sleep with it anymore? Maybe he has a new favorite—it's not like I would really know. Even when I'm at home, I'm never the one putting him to bed. Never the one reading him the same bedtime story every day for weeks on end, or making sure he has his sippy cup of water on his nightstand.

They all stopped asking me to a long time ago, and it's not like I volunteer.

I creep into his room, which is bathed in a soft yellow glow of the nightlight by his bed. He's huddled up in the corner of his bed, smooshed up against the wall like usual. Despite how uncomfortable it looks, it's how he's always wanted to sleep. Dad jokes that Ty is like a cat with a cardboard box—the smaller the space he can fit into, the happier he is.

His blond wispy hair is mussed, his little eyelids fluttering in sleep. I don't see another stuffed animal next to (or under) him, so I set it on the bed next to his hand. So if he reaches out for it in the night, it'll be there.

If it would even matter to him. I don't know.

Then I go back to my own bedroom, wishing I had something to reach for as I slept. Or maybe someone. I strip down, pull on a Ben Folds concert t-shirt I like to sleep in, and crawl into bed, remembering how Felix smiled for *me*. Remembering the way he turned me down for sex, because he wants me to be his girlfriend first. How he said he wants to take me to prom and how he held me in his arms like I was something precious, something worth holding on to.

No, he's definitely not like the other guys I screw around with. And the last thing I want to do is mess things up for him.

Except maybe that isn't exactly true. I'm selfish, after all.

The last thing I want to do right now is give him up.

I can't help but notice the prom posters all over school the next day—cheesy, glitter-lettered signs plastered around the walls of the outdoor courtyards and above the lockers of the indoor hallways. The signs have been there for a couple weeks already, but I've done my best to ignore them.

Now my eyes catch on every one.

I'm at school earlier than most days, though still late enough for my first class—PE—that I'm not even going to poke my head in the gym. Partly my earlier arrival is because my new robot child woke me up crying at both four AM and again at seven-thirty. But if I'm being honest, I just want to see Felix again.

Which is crazy stupid, I tell myself, jiggling the animatronic kid nervously. Probably he already regrets last night. Probably he's going to have walked into these halls—on time, because he's Felix Mays—and come back to his senses and know what a terrible idea it was to think I'd make a good girlfriend.

He'll be glad I didn't agree to that, that I didn't let him throw away his golden boy social status by publicly *dating* me. Maybe he'll regret not sleeping with me when he had the chance, but he'll wonder what the hell he was thinking wanting more than that from the school slut.

Except.

I can't shake the way he looked at me when he called me beautiful. The way he said my name, breathless, his eyes locked on mine, with my lips inches away from his. The way his voice sounded when he asked if he had a chance with me, taut with that same fear and exhilaration that was coursing through me like some heady new pill.

And I can't help but believe it was real, and that he meant it then, and still means it today.

The last time I was this nervous walking through school, I'd just come back after having Ty. I remember the way everyone looked at me, the whispers, the muffled laughs. I was already pretty well known to be a skank—it was how I got pregnant by some random college guy, after all—but this just cemented it. I wasn't me anymore, I was a walking scarlet letter, and the best way I knew how to get by was to act like I was actually *two* walking letters—F and U.

If I didn't care about what anyone thought, ever, then nothing they thought could hurt me. I was already pretty well practiced at that.

Today is different. Because I do care what Felix thinks of me. I have since I started listening to him play, and after last night, I can't even pretend to myself anymore that I don't.

I draw in a breath, at least forcing myself to walk like I don't give a shit. Even though there's not really anyone in the hallways to fool.

At least until I reach my locker and see my friend Ian leaning against it, his black hair flopping over his face while he texts. Probably setting up a meet somewhere. He deals in prescription pills, E, some pot—that kind of thing. I've never bought from him personally; I actually don't buy drugs at all. I'm not into the heavy stuff, and for the most part, being a cute girl at parties gets you pills or a joint for free whenever you want them.

He looks up when he hears the click of my heeled boots on the linoleum.

"Hey," he says, and he's got a weird grin on his face.

"What's up with you?" I ask, looking around. "Why are you staking out my locker?"

He shrugs. He's wearing his usual long black coat with the over-sized lapels that makes him look like he's in some pirate mafia. I've always thought it looks a little over-the-top goth, like he got dressed blindly in the back of a Hot Topic, but I like to wear corsets and put my hair up in spiky buns, so who am I to judge?

"Maybe I just want to see your reaction when you look inside," he says. I would say he's trying to sound innocent, but Ian sucks at innocent.

I narrow my eyes. "What did you put in my locker?"

"*I* didn't put anything in there. But I did give your combination to Felix Mays."

My heart slams against my ribcage. "You—why did you do that?"

"Because he had something for you." Ian smirks. "And it's not like I haven't seen you checking him out all year."

I gape, and then snap my mouth shut and settle for a glare at Ian. Dammit, I thought I'd actually kept my stupid fantasies a better secret than that. But I guess Ian knows me fairly well—he's pretty much my only real friend, even if that friendship mainly revolves around gross cafeteria lunches and hitting up the same parties. Despite what everyone thinks, we've never slept together. It's just not a thing for us, even though we're both straight and easy. It's kind of nice, having a guy friend who I know doesn't expect anything like that from me. I think he feels the same, but I wouldn't really know. It's not like we talk about stuff like that.

The bell rings, and I actually jump, which makes his smirk even more smug and my glare at him more vicious. Kids start spilling out into the hallways, the noise level going from nothing to chaos almost instantly.

"Come on, open it. You don't want to be late for class," Ian says. Like being late for class has ever been a concern of mine.

Except maybe today, with a certain health class.

My palms are sweaty as I work the combination. Maybe it's a note, saying he changed his mind. Saying it was all a joke. I try to prepare myself for that, like it'll make it hurt less.

The locker pops open. Inside is a long-stemmed rose sitting on top of my pile of books. I pull it out, gingerly. All the thorns have been cut off, and its petals are big and velvety and deep red.

No guy has ever given me a flower before.

"Awww, how sweet." Ian's voice drips with sarcasm. "The boy's a true romantic."

"Shut up," I shoot back, slamming my locker closed and walking away from him. But I hold the rose tight as I walk, my steps feeling lighter than ever before, and I try to ignore how many heads turn at the sight of Jenna Rollins carrying a rose and a robot baby and grinning like an idiot.

FIVE

Felix

book it to health class as soon as the bell rings, so I'm the third person to the room. I take my seat and wait, my palms sweating.

Last night I made out with Jenna Rollins, and the kissing was better than all the sex I've had combined. I spent most of last night reliving it in my dreams—which went a lot farther than we did in reality. Still, the heat of last night is cut with a cold undercurrent today. What if Jenna was just messing with me? She didn't say she'd be my girlfriend. She didn't actually say she'd go to prom with me. She didn't agree to anything I asked for except making out in the dirt lot, when she probably could have gone to that party instead and hooked up with college guys.

Also, I realized this morning I'd forgotten to get the baby from her last night. I hope she hasn't left it at home today. I hope even more she shows up to class at all.

The room is still mostly empty when Jenna appears in the doorway. My heart taps out a tympani rhythm as her eyes meet mine. She's holding our baby under one arm and the rose I left in her locker in the other hand, and looking as terrified as I am.

I smile at her, and she smiles shyly back. And then we're both grinning like complete idiots. She strides over to her desk—she's wearing a sparkly silver skirt today with knee-high boots and a black corset. I'm remembering what it felt like to run my hands up the backs of her thighs as she sits sideways in her seat and crosses her legs in my direction. She holds out the baby. "I think you forgot this," she says softly.

I'm a bit surprised she isn't announcing to the entire class—who are filing in more rapidly as we get closer to the bell—that I was at her house last night. It seems like the sort of brash thing she would do.

"Nice flower," I say. "Secret admirer?"

Her cheeks blush pink. "I guess so."

We smile at each other for a long moment, until Brett Walter comes and sits in his desk right between us. Then Jenna turns toward the front of the classroom, but I can still see her holding her rose, brushing the soft petals against her lips.

A shiver runs through me, remembering how soft they were, how she felt on top of me, the way she laughed when we talked between bouts of kissing.

At the front of the classroom, Daniel is staring back at me, his face turning red again. I don't know if that's because he's putting things together or because he's embarrassed by the thought of me *talking* to a girl, which I'm guessing he has to do at least minimally with his own partner. I raise an eyebrow at him and give him a smug smile, just to mess with him.

He turns rapidly back around in his seat.

Class crawls by, interrupted frequently by the crying of babies. I put mine up on my shoulder and pat it half-heartedly while Ms. Crandall drones on about the effects of drugs and alcohol on unborn babies.

I'm pretty sure Jenna does drugs at the parties she goes to, and I'm certain she drinks. I wonder if she was doing that when she got pregnant, or if the partying came later. I don't know much about any of that, I realize. Only what I've heard around school.

"Dude," Jason says from behind me. "How's your crack

43

baby? Does it have fetal alcohol syndrome?"

A couple of girls giggle behind me, and I whip around and glare at him. "Shut up," I say.

Jason looks at me wide-eyed. He's right to. Before yesterday I would have just shrugged that off, or laughed along with. Hell, yesterday I was the one *making* the jokes, which feels horrifying now. "Dude," he says. "Don't take it personally. You're probably not even the father."

I glare hard at him, my fingers twitching on the back of the seat. I know I shouldn't hit him, for lots of reasons. First, because Jason Amala plays football and could kick my ass any day. Second, because we're in the middle of health class. Third, because as much as Jenna would mock me for this, I really can't afford to damage my hands. And fourth, because I've never hit anyone in my life unless you count whacking my sister Gabby with a toy light saber when we were little, and I'd probably suck at it.

"Shut. Up." I repeat.

"Felix Mays," Ms. Crandall says, and I swing back around. The whole class is looking at me, and I'm not sure if that started when Ms. Crandall called my name, or before. "Is there a problem?"

Jenna is looking at me with some mix of fear and shame on her face, and her rose has disappeared under her desk. I want to reach across Brett and touch her, let her know that it's okay. We're okay.

All right, maybe it's me who wants to know that things are okay.

"No," I say. "No problem."

Behind me, I hear Jason whisper something, and I'm glad I don't make out the words. There are more giggles from behind him, but Ms. Crandall goes back to the lecture.

After a few minutes, Jenna reaches past Brett and tosses a torn piece of notebook paper onto my desk. I cover it with my hand, and then turn it over. The last thing I want is this read to the class.

Don't feel like you have to defend me, it says.

Jenna's not looking back at me, and I'm not sure how to

respond. I do feel like I have to defend her, but not out of obligation. I'm angry with myself for being the person everyone thinks is in on these jokes. I hate that yesterday, I was.

I slide a piece of paper out of my notebook and write a response, and then reach past Brett's arm and brush it against Jenna's bare shoulder. She takes it in her hand, but just then Ms. Crandall looks up and sees me letting it go, and Jenna taking it.

Shit.

"Mr. Mays," Ms. Crandall says. "What is it that's so important you have to interrupt the class?"

"Just arranging childcare schedules," I tell her. "Passing notes so as *not* to interrupt the class."

Ms. Crandall's eyes harden, and she holds out her hand. "Jenna Rollins," she says. "I'll take that."

Jenna gives me an alarmed look, as if she's wondering if she should swallow the note rather than relinquish it, and I shake my head and shrug, like it's fine.

Ms. Crandall opens the note. "*What if I want to?*" she reads to the class. The room erupts in giggles as our classmates imagine what it is I might want to do with Jenna Rollins. "Good to see you're taking an active role in fatherhood, Felix." More giggles. I know I should smile, to play it off. But Jenna's face has hardened back to its usual shell of bare tolerance and perpetual malaise, and all I want is to hold her again like I did last night and remind her that not everyone in this school is an asshole.

Except I have been. I've been participating in doing this to her, and now everyone expects me to play along.

The lecture finally ends, and Ms. Crandall sets up her computer to monitor our kids. We're to fill out some worksheet about alcohol consumption that basically asks over and over again how much alcohol is safe to use in various circumstances—when pregnant, when driving, when under age. They don't want actual answers—clearly we're supposed to say that it's never safe under any of these circumstances, whether that's medically true or not.

"Daniel and Angela," Ms. Crandall calls, and Angela brings up their squealing kid while Daniel lingers four feet behind her like he doesn't want to admit that he's got a robot baby, even though everyone knows he didn't have actual robot sex to get it.

When Brett gets up with his partner, I lean forward and put a hand on Jenna's arm. She jumps, but when she turns around to look at me, her mask of disinterest is still on.

"You okay?" I ask.

She shrugs one shoulder, as if the situation doesn't rise to the importance of meriting two. "Why wouldn't I be?"

She spins back around before I can say anything else, which is just as well, because the people sitting around us are starting to stare. The rumor that something's going on between us is going to spread like crazy, and I don't care except that it's probably going to make things harder for Jenna.

"Felix and Jenna!" Ms. Crandall calls, and I pick up the kid and head to the front of the classroom. Jenna stays in her seat as Ms. Crandall unsnaps the pajamas—which were apparently once worn by the kid I met yesterday, Ty. It's hard to believe that grinning, bouncing, cape-wearing boy was ever that small, but I suppose we all were, once.

I'm afraid Jenna's going to ignore me, that maybe I came on too strong with the rose, that maybe she's decided she's done with me. But when I turn around, she's stood up from her desk and come over. As she steps up next to me, her fingers brush mine, so slightly it could have been accidental.

My body heats up. I'm pretty sure it wasn't.

"Ninety-four percent," Ms. Crandall says. "Well done."

Jenna smirks at me and rubs her fingers together. I nod. I have the cash and will pay up after class. No way did I think that making out with her meant I was getting out of that.

When class is over, Jenna books it out like she always does, but I find her waiting for me out in the hall. I hand over the money, and she smiles. "You got out of baby duty last night, but you're taking her tonight." She reaches out and takes the baby off my shoulder, her hands brushing against my shirt as she does.

I reach a hand out, resting it on her hip, wanting to pull her into me and kiss her and kiss her like I did last night. I think Jenna can tell, because she gives me a coy smile, and purses her lips just slightly before spinning around and stalking off down the hallway. People around me are staring again, but all I can do is stand there with a stupid look on my face and watch her as she walks away.

By lunch I've already had several people ask me what's going on with me and Jenna Rollins, including Julia's friend Angela, who I'm pretty sure is only asking as a proxy. I shrug at each of them and say that we're partners for the baby project. There are enough babies around school that everyone knows what that means—different class periods have been taking their turns for weeks. I grab school lunch at the counter—I'm always too lazy to pack my own—and move through the cafeteria. I can see my friends gathered at our usual table. Julia is there, and she's looking right at me. As soon as I sit down, I'm going to be asked a million questions. I can already tell.

But instead, I walk over to the table where Jenna is sitting. Ian is there again, but I already know he's okay, because he gave me Jenna's locker combination when I flagged him down this morning before school. I bring my tray over and slide onto the bench beside Jenna.

"Hey," I say.

Jenna looks up at me with a lot more surprise than she afforded me yesterday. "Hi," she says. "Isn't your lunch table over there?" She indicates in the direction of my friends, who are all staring in my direction now, and Julia looks like she's ready to set something on fire.

"Maybe. Am I not allowed to sit here?"

Jenna looks at Ian across the table, and he returns an amused smile. He's clearly enjoying watching her squirm. I think he might like me, and I take that as a small victory.

"Eat wherever you want," Jenna says. Her tone is harsh, and for a second, I think I've made a mistake. But the rose from her locker is poking out of the zipper of her backpack, the edges of the petals bruised from too much handling. Her hand brushes mine under the table.

She wants me here. I stick a french fry into some ketchup and lean my elbow on the table.

Across the cafeteria, some of my friends are now whispering to each other, and this guy David who plays first chair clarinet is waving at me like, what the hell are you doing?

I shrug and take Jenna's hand under the table. She lets me.

"You're going to pay for this, you know," she says.

I eye the baby, resting on the table top, mercifully quiet for the moment. "I know. A hundred dollars a day."

She shakes her head. "Not that. Although you are still paying me for that."

"As long as we get a ninety percent."

"But you're going to lose a whole lot more being seen with me."

I look up at Ian, but he's playing with his phone now, staying out of it. I'm glad he's here, though. He's a big guy, and he makes it a lot less likely that anyone's going to come over and harass us right here. Jenna seems like she might be one nasty comment away from deciding I'm not worth it, and that scares the hell out of me.

"I've got nothing to lose," I say.

Jenna laughs. "How can you say that? You're the golden boy. Everyone loves you. You have everything to lose."

"Maybe I don't care what other people think."

"Maybe you will, when they're asking you in the halls if you have syphilis."

My stomach drops, and I squeeze her hand. "I really am

sorry about that. I know the apology doesn't change it, but—"

"Whatever," Jenna says. "It's fine." Though I know it isn't. We established last night that I hurt her feelings. "But I'm just saying, you might want to think about everything you're throwing away."

"I'm not throwing away anything I care about," I say. "They can't do anything to me. If they're going to be jerks about the girl I'm dating, they weren't really my friends to begin with."

Ian raises his eyebrows at Jenna over the dating comment, but Jenna ignores him.

"Yeah, okay," Jenna says. "But you get a lot of respect around here, and—"

"I get respect because I'm the best damn musician in the school." I wince. For all I know *Jenna* is the best damn musician in the school. But my point stands. "And no one can do anything about that. I'm the first chair cello, and I'm always going to be first chair cello. Mr. Geist doesn't give a crap who I'm dating, as long as I keep playing better than anyone else. And I will."

Jenna looks up at me, like she wants to argue with that, but she can't.

"Besides," Ian says, "he's a guy. People are going to think he's badass for banging you."

"Yeah," I say. "Sorry about that."

Jenna shakes her head like she can't imagine the benefits to my reputation are going to outweigh the costs, and she's probably right. Especially when I start getting in fights with assholes who call her a crack whore to my face.

"Did it bother you when I defended you?" I ask.

Both Ian and Jenna look surprised.

"I just don't want you to feel like you have to," she says. "I have a reputation for a reason. Most of the stuff they say about me is true."

I believe that, since last night she was trying to convince me to have sex with her by the side of the road. And I guess that's supposed to bother me, that she's been with a bunch of other guys, and I guess may continue to do so, since she's not my girlfriend.

Okay, that last part does bother me.

"I don't care if it's true," I say. "I don't want people thinking they can insult the girl I'm dating, and I'm going to just laugh along with them."

Jenna looks up at me, her eyes searching mine. "You won't?"

My heart aches that she has to ask this. I wish so badly I hadn't said all that shit yesterday. "Never," I tell her. I look down at her lips, and I think I've given her ample warning to pull away before my lips brush hers.

But she scoots away from me, like I've burned her. "Don't do that," she says.

My hands go cold. Ian is looking between Jenna and me like we're some puzzle he can't quite figure out. I can hardly blame him for that.

Jenna's dropped my hand, and I rub my palms together. I've pushed this too far. She doesn't actually want to be with me. I was probably some adventure she was having, dating the orchestra nerd, and she was contemplating going to prom with me as part of the experience. And the stupid thing is, I still want to do that with her, even if that's all it is. I want to be the guy who gives her that, even if that's all she'll let me give her.

"I'm sorry," I say. "I'll back off."

Jenna shakes her head, like this isn't what she wants, and now I'm as confused as Ian is. "I just don't want to drag you down with me," she says.

"I've already told you what I want," I tell her.

She looks up at me, and there's relief in her eyes. I realize then that maybe she thought I was having second thoughts, about prom, about her being my girlfriend.

"Jenna Rollins playing hard to get," Ian says. "Never thought I'd see the day."

"Shut up," Jenna says with a little laugh, and I smile.

But I don't think this is some game we're playing. I think that's why she's scared to trust it, and if I'm being honest, so am I.

When we finish eating, Jenna pulls me out to the abandoned sports field and we slip into the dugout on the softball diamond and kiss up against the plywood wall. Jenna's body writhes against mine as we devour each other, and I want to lift her up and make love to her right there against the wall.

Not that I have experience doing it like that, and she probably does, and I don't know what I'm doing, and that alone is enough to make me keep my promise not to sleep with her unless she's my girlfriend. I can tell she wants more, though, and so do I.

I rest my hands on her shoulders, prying us apart, even though my body hates me for it. "Hey," I say. "What is this we're doing? Are we dating in secret?"

Jenna shrugs. "Don't you want to?"

"Date you, yes. Be your secret? Not really." I hesitate. "I know this is stupid, but I'm starting to feel like you're the one who doesn't want to ruin your reputation."

Jenna's eyes harden, and I feel like I've made a mistake. She opens her mouth, and I cringe inwardly, expecting her to yell at me.

"You really still want that," she says. "Even though you know what people say about me. What they're going to say about you."

The tightness in my chest eases. On my backpack on the bench behind us, our baby whines.

"Well, we do have a kid together," I say. "So some of the reputation is earned."

Jenna smiles, and lays her head on my chest. "I suppose we do."

I run a hand up her back. "Can I ask you something personal?"

She nods.

"Who is Ty's father?"

She turns into me, her face pressed against my shirt. "I don't know. Some guy at a frat party."

I nod, but something about that bothers me. I know she goes to college parties now, but—

"You were fourteen," I say. "At a frat party."

"I know. Not my finest decision."

But that's not what bothers me about it. It's one thing for

51

Jenna to be doing that now. Most of her class is eighteen by now, so if she's not, she's close. But when she was just a kid—

"They had to know you were underage," I say.

"They did. But I looked old for my age, so they didn't know how young I was."

Still. That's statutory rape, and I want to punch every guy in whatever frat house she went to in the face.

"Let me take you out," I say. "On a date, somewhere public. Today."

Jenna's arms tighten around me, and I squeeze her back, just enjoying the feel of her in my arms. "Are you sure you want to do that?" she asks.

"Yes," I tell her. "More than anything."

"I think lunch is probably over. You're going to be late to class."

"Let's skip class." I'm not going to learn anything anyway. I won't be able to think about anything but her.

Jenna looks up at me with mock surprise. "Felix Mays wants to skip class?"

"I skip class sometimes," I say.

She arches an eyebrow at me.

"Okay, usually to practice. But sometimes for other reasons."

"I'm a bad influence on you," Jenna says.

"No. You're making me happier than I can ever remember, and I want to earn my keep."

Jenna laughs, and it's as beautiful as it was last night. I run a hand along her cheek. "I'll take you anywhere," I say. "It's your first real date, since making out in a car hardly counts. Name the place."

Jenna is quiet for a long moment. "Disneyland," she says. Her eyes are dancing, and she's clearly challenging me, and I do some quick calculations. Disneyland is crazy expensive, but my parents give me a decent allowance every month to cover clothes, music, school fees, gas, and whatever I want to do for fun. I'm not a big spender, except on music, so I've saved up quite a bit of it.

"I don't know," I say. "Childcare is eating up a lot of my funds."

Jenna smiles and shakes her head. "Damn price-gouging nannies. I hope you're at least getting sex out of it."

I laugh, and feel her heart beating against me. I have the money. I won't have much left after this week is done, but I don't care.

"Okay," I say. "Let's do it."

Jenna looks up at me. "Have sex?"

"Go to Disneyland." It's a drive from here, but doable. And I can make up an excuse for my parents about needing to practice.

"What about your four hours of cello?" Jenna asks.

"I think I can skip just this once," I tell her. I don't tell her I'll play an extra two hours on both Saturday and Sunday to make up for it. I do that occasionally, when I can't get all my hours in, or when I need some extra practice for All-State philharmonic.

"You're not serious," Jenna says.

But I am. "Come on," I say, and I lead her by the hand out to the parking lot where we climb in my car and I set my GPS to take us to Anaheim. And when Jenna sees I'm serious, she smiles like she can't believe this is happening.

I know exactly how she feels.

SIX

Jenna

We're actually here at Disneyland. He said he'd take me anywhere, and so I'd suggested the most ridiculous place I could think of that was still technically possible—not thinking for a minute he'd actually go for that.

Who takes a girl—a girl like me, no less—on a first date to Disneyland?

Felix Mays, apparently. I look over at him again as we stand in line for Big Thunder Mountain Railway, and grin. I can't seem to stop doing that. Looking *or* grinning.

He purses his lips and studies me, then nods. "Okay, I've come to a decision."

My pulse quickens. A decision? About me?

About us?

I lean back against the fake log railing, hoping he can't see how tight my grip on it is. "Yeah?"

"Yeah. I spent the whole drive here trying to decide if you actually like Disneyland, or if you just like it ironically."

Relief trickles through me, and I give him a coy look. "Is that really what you spent the whole drive here thinking about?"

His cheeks flush a little, even as he gives me a knowing look back. I wonder if he's remembering the feel of my hand on his leg as he drove—I know I am. It took everything in me not to keep inching it up higher, if only to see how adorably flustered he'd get. "Well, maybe that's not *all* I thought about."

I tug on his shirt, pulling him closer, and he doesn't resist, his hands finding my waist, his head tilted down to mine. "So what did you decide?" I ask, even though what I really want is to press my lips to his and not stop until we're on the damn rollercoaster—and maybe not even then.

He smiles like he can read my thoughts. "There's nothing ironic about it. I think you actually like it. No, scratch that. I think you *love* it. I think you're a secret Disney nerd, like you come here on weekends and trade pins and find the hidden Mickeys and stuff."

His eyes are so close to mine, so blue and deep. His lips inches away. "Really. *That's* how I spend my weekends?"

"Yep. And you were signaling it all along." He flicks his gaze up, to my hair. "The Mickey ears."

I burst out laughing, and he grins, like he's won some little victory—it's the way he smiles every time he makes me laugh like that, and I wonder if he can't get enough of my laugh the way I can't get enough of that smile. Or of him.

Don't hope for things someone like you can't really have, part of me whispers. *Don't be stupid.*

Except I'm starting to wonder if maybe feeling this way about him—even if it doesn't make sense, even if it defies everything I've come to believe about myself—maybe that's not stupid. Maybe the only stupid thing would be to pretend it doesn't exist.

The dad with three chattering little girls standing behind us in line clears his throat, and for a second I think maybe he's worried Felix and I are standing so close to each other that we're going to go at it against the railing right here in front of his kids, but then I see he's just trying to let us know the line has moved again. Or maybe it's a bit of both.

I tug Felix forward and we move up a dozen steps or so, and

I lean back against the railing again.

"You got me," I say, and I feel my own cheeks warming. I at once both hope he gets how much I really mean that—in a way that has nothing to do with my non-ironic love of Disneyland—and hope that he really, really doesn't.

He resumes his place close up against me, standing between my legs. I'm wearing jeans now, so it's not quite as inappropriate a picture for a family-friendly park as it would have been in my short silver skirt. Before we drove to Disney, we stopped at my place first so I could change into pants and sneakers—I love the way those boots make my legs look, but I'm not about to walk Disneyland for hours in heels that high.

I kept the corset on, though, and my slim black jeans ride low enough on my hips that an inch or so of stomach shows above them. Family attraction or not, I'm not about to dress like a nun. Or Rachel.

He's watching me carefully, like he really is trying to discern what I meant by that, and I chicken out.

"I mean, you're a little right."

"A *little*." He sighs in mock sorrow. "A word every guy wants applied to him. In any capacity."

I smile. Felix isn't exactly a big guy overall, but I'm definitely not worried about *that*. I got a pretty good sense from straddling him in the car last night.

"Well, in the capacity of you figuring out my deep dark secret, it applies." I hook my fingers through the belt loops of his jeans, just up under his shirt, and tug on them lightly. "I do actually like Disneyland, for real. But I haven't been since I was like eleven. So there's no pins, no princess costumes at home. No hidden hair messages."

"Damn," he says. "It felt like a good explanation for the buns."

I feign hurt. "Are you saying you don't like them?"

"I do like them. Like probably way more than I should for such a crazy-ass hairstyle." He reaches up with both hands and squeezes them, and I laugh.

"Stop groping my buns, you perv."

"You have no idea how long I've wanted to do that."

The idea of him sitting two seats behind me in health class all year, longing to squeeze my *hair* makes me happier than it has any right to—especially because I'm not sure how actually true it is.

"So you really haven't been here since you were eleven?" he asks, his hands sliding down along my arms and raising little goosebumps in their wake.

"It's kind of out of my family's price range," I say dryly, then regret it when he winces a little. I don't want him to feel bad for coming from more money than me—it is what it is, as they say. I don't get the feeling he cares much that my clothes are thrift store finds rather than designer label—if he even notices that sort of thing, which a lot of kids at our high school do—or what part of town I live in. But I also don't want to remind him even more of all the differences between us.

"I used to go once a year, though," I say, trying to steer the topic away a bit. "My grandparents live in Michigan, but every summer before my grandma died, they'd fly out and take Rachel and me here. My grandma was terrified of roller coasters, so she'd never go on any of the big rides. But I remember one year, we convinced her to go on this one, Thunder Mountain. We told her it was a kid's ride."

Felix looks around at the line behind us, mostly filled with parents and fairly small kids. "Which it is."

"Exactly. But oh my god, the minute this thing is going over the first drop, my grandma—who is like this sweet, devout religious lady—lets out this super loud 'Oh shit!' and continues to swear like a dirty beat cop the whole ride. And Rachel and I were just busting up laughing. You should have seen the looks she got from all the other parents."

Felix laughs, and we move along with the line. "My parents would never go on the rides, either. They actually weren't big on bringing us here. Probably because my mom worried someone might see her having fun with the masses. But my oldest sister Dana brought my other sister Gabby and me here a couple times, and that was pretty fun. Even though it involved Dana."

I smile, but my stomach clenches. Is he serious about his mom? Is she one of those rich lady society types? I can't imagine she'll be thrilled by her son dating me. Or taking me to prom. If that's still happening. Not that I've ever cared before what some guy's mom thinks of me.

But there are a lot of things different about Felix.

"So your sister—" I start, but a muffled wailing sound interrupts me. Our baby, which is currently crammed into Felix's backpack.

He sighs and takes her out and starts patting her back. When she calms down, I take his backpack and wedge his sweatshirt down to the bottom and put the baby in, zipping it up so her head pokes out the top. "Here," I say, "It's like a baby carrier. Wear it in front."

He laughs and does so, then adjusts her so her arms are sticking straight up. "There. She's ready for the rides."

He looks hilarious, and so of course I have to take a pic, and then we do a selfie of the two of us with our backpack baby. And then we're at the front of the line, and he takes my hand and we ride the rollercoaster together, screaming louder than I think either of us actually needs to and I'm dying laughing because he's mouthing swear words at me on every drop.

We spend hours at the park like this—riding the rides, hanging out in lines, our hands as all over each other as they can be while not forcing any parents to give their kids "the talk" right here at the park. We laugh at our Splash Mountain picture and make jokes about our baby meeting her animatronic cousins on It's a Small World. I tell him about other Disney memories with my grandparents and Rachel, like the time she got so excited about the Dumbo ride she threw up *in line*. He tells me similarly embarrassing stories about his sisters, especially Gabby, who is three years older than him and clearly the favorite sister of the two. He doesn't talk much about his parents, and I'm scared to ask.

I don't think any guy's parents would approve of their son dating me. What I don't know—and am afraid to find out—is how much that will ultimately matter to him.

That new source of anxiety aside, the whole afternoon is the most fun I've had in . . . well, I don't know. A long time. Maybe ever. Hanging out with Felix like this is both crazy giddy—my nerves alight with every touch, my pulse racing every time those blue eyes of his crinkle at the sides as he smiles—and weirdly comfortable. Like the thick layer of wary disregard I drape around myself with guys—with everyone, really—is lighter than air, and just as transparent. Like I am somehow more truly myself today, with him, than I've ever been.

This sense of comfort doesn't make me want to jump him any less, though. On the Haunted Mansion ride, in the dark and relative privacy of our little seat, we make out like we did in the softball dugout, feverishly and full of need, our bodies as tangled as they can be with clothes and the ride bar in the way. I want him so badly I ache with it.

But not just sex. I want *him*. I want this, and us, holding hands in the hallway of school. Making out against the lockers between class. Me, sitting in the orchestra room with him after school, instead of out in the hallway by myself. Watching him play. Having him smile at me while he does so. Us, curled up in bed, falling asleep to each other's heartbeats. Waking up to see him there, still holding me. Feeling safe. Loved.

The ride ends, and we exit, with that last word echoing in my head, stealing my breath even more than our furious make-out session of moments before.

Am I in *love* with Felix?

Panic rips through me at even the question. I'm not the girl that gets the guy—not for more than a quickie at a party or in the backseat of a car. I'm the girl who goes to parties and gets so drunk she blacks out. I'm the girl who is awful to her family, who goes out with the guy her sister has a crush on and then rubs it in her face.

I've seen the movies, read the books, and they pretty much all agree—I'm not the girl who gets the love story.

"Hey, are you okay?" Felix looks concerned as we make our way past the vendor selling *Nightmare Before Christmas* merch. It's only then that I realize I dropped his hand as we left the mansion, that I'm walking farther away from him than I have all day. He wets his lips. "Did I do something that made you uncomfortable? I didn't mean to. I'm sorry."

It's not just concern; he looks straight-up scared, and I feel like the worst person ever. For so many reasons.

I stop walking and turn to face him. "Rachel likes you." It comes out sounding like an accusation, but he's not really the one I'm accusing.

He blinks. Clearly he wasn't expecting this. "Okay," he says. "*Okay?*"

"I mean, I'm not into your sister, if that's what you're wondering." He's giving me this confused look, and I can't really blame him. "I'd have thought that was pretty obvious by now."

It is, but that's not the problem. "Why not? Rachel's pretty and smart and she cares about people, and she cares about her future. She's a good person."

I realize I'm pretty much parroting back all the things Rachel said about him. Which were all true.

His brow furrows. "Rachel's great, sure. She seems cool, and I'd like to be friends with her, but not—I mean, she's kind of young."

I raise my eyebrow at him. "Yeah, a whole grade younger. Because who would do that?"

I'm going for caustic irony, because well, obviously *I* would, but he blanches, like I struck a nerve. I feel even worse, but I have no idea what to say.

Apparently he doesn't either. There's a long moment of silence, and then he edges closer to me. He still has that scared look on his face, like I'm some feral animal that needs to be approached carefully. And hell, maybe I am. "What is this really about? Do you feel bad dating me if your sister likes me?"

I study my sneakers, my arms wrapped tightly around myself because I'm worried if I let go I'll wrap my arms around *him*.

"Because I'm not into Rachel," he says, taking my silence for the unfortunate admission it is. "Not at all. Definitely not like this." He touches my elbow, lightly. "Even if you and I weren't— even if I'd never met you. I wouldn't be into her like that."

"Maybe it would be better for you if you were," I say, still staring down at my shoes. "Into her, or someone more like her, you know?"

"Well maybe you don't get to decide who I like." His tone is a little pissy, something I haven't heard from him since that first night at my house.

Which was last night. Oh my god, how was that only last night? How do I feel like *this* about him already?

How much deeper in this will I be by this time tomorrow?

"Look, I'm sorry," he says with a sigh, staring down at his own shoes. "But I think you *are* good for me. I think—"

"How? What is it you like about me?" The words tumble out of my mouth, another accusation. "What makes you want to date *me*?" I'm pretty sure the way I'm handling *this* particular conversation isn't the reason.

He gapes a bit, then looks like he's about to answer, when a baby wails.

Damn robot baby, I think, and we both look at each other— and have the realization at the same time.

Neither one of us has the backpack. Or our baby.

"Oh shit," Felix says, looking around the path behind us, as if maybe our baby is going to be found toddling along behind us, dragging Felix's Jansport behind her.

"Oh my god, we lost our child at Disneyland," I groan.

I don't particularly care about my grade, but I know Felix does, and though this is not my fault alone—it takes two to get so distracted making out on rides that we leave our baby on some roller coaster—it feels like one more reason why being with me is not great for him.

Someone like Rachel wouldn't have forgotten the kid, even if she was making out with Felix Mays.

"Did we have it on the Haunted Mansion?" Felix asks.

"I last remember her on Splash Mountain. That second time. Because I said that thing about wondering if we should be taking our android child on a water ride, or if that's like reckless endangerment, and—"

"And I shoved her back in the backpack," he says, face-palming. "And that was like two rides ago. Shit."

We run back to the Haunted Mansion first, finding an employee willing to go check the ride, only to verify that, no, no child has been left behind, robot or otherwise. She recommends we check with guest services at the front of the park. "Or," she says, a little smugly. "You could go to the 'lost parent zone' at Town Hall."

I resist the very strong urge to flip her off. We check another ride we went on, the spinning teacups, but no luck there, either.

"Look," I say, as we walk briskly along main street, dodging families in a long line to get an autograph from Princess Jasmine. "If we can't find the baby, I'll take the blame for it."

"What?" He looks back at me and slows down. The worry line in his forehead deepens even more. "No. Why would—"

"Because there's no reason to ruin your grade. Mine's already crap. I'll tell Mrs. Crandall I kidnapped our child and sold it on the robot baby black market for weed."

The worry line eases a bit as he fights a smile. "That's the story you're going with?"

"You don't think she'd believe it?"

"I didn't say that. I just think you're likely to have to repeat health class." *Again*, I can tell he thinks, but doesn't say.

"Doubtful. Principal Evans is counting down the days until me and my 'flagrant dress code and behavior violations' are no longer his problem."

His smile is a little sad, though I'm not sure why. But he takes my hand again, his fingers threaded through mine, and it feels so good that he wants to, even after my little freak-out—which I'm still all tense from—that it makes me a little dizzy.

"If we lose it," he says, squeezing my hand, "we'll tell my dad that the baby got stolen and this will jeopardize my grade and thus my future, and I'll get a lecture about responsibility, after which he'll proceed to cut the school a check to ensure they can buy a dozen more babies. Or one baby with its own private security team."

"Yeah, okay." I smile, despite how my stomach still feels all knotted up. "I suppose we could go that way."

We keep walking, less urgently now, even though I'm still hoping against hope that we find this kid. I really don't want Felix to have to get his parents involved—especially given that I'm worried for them to even know I exist, let alone already causing trouble in their son's life. And also, the baby was wearing Ty's outfit, and the thought of losing that is—

A thought hits me like a fist to the gut, hard enough it stops me in my tracks.

"Ty," I say softly.

Felix stops, too, tethered to me by our linked fingers. "What about him?" Then his expression falls. "Oh, god, Ty's pajamas— they're like special, aren't they? Because they were his."

Something warms in my chest, knowing Felix somehow understands this, without me ever saying anything.

"Yeah, they are," I say, my cheeks burning. Because, really, what right do I have to be attached to something of Ty's? "But it's not just that." My throat is tight, and of all the admissions I've blurted out to Felix today, this is the one I'm most afraid for him, or anyone, to know.

"I've been here at Disneyland for hours now," I say, fighting to get the words out, because god, *I* don't want to hear them. "Like making jokes about our baby, and being surrounded by little kids and—" I swallow, my eyes burning. "I *have* a kid who would have loved this. But I didn't even think about bringing him. I didn't think about him at all. Not once."

Felix looks stricken, and the cracks webbing my heart splinter further. He grips my hand tighter. "I didn't think about it either."

"Yeah, but he's *my kid*. And I didn't even think about him—here, of all places!" I shake my head, blinking back the stupid tears I refuse to cry. I've spent years refusing to cry, and I'm not about to start now. "It's probably good I didn't think to bring him. I would've forgotten *him* on some fucking ride."

"No, you wouldn't have." Felix sounds so sure, and after a long beat, I nod.

"No, I wouldn't have." Not because I'm such a great mom or even babysitter. But because when Ty's around me, I'm always hyper-aware of him. Anxious in a way I can't explain, my eyes tracking every little movement, my nerves raw at every cry or even happy toddler babble.

Afraid, I think, that he'll need me for something, and I won't be able to give it to him. That I'll never be able to.

Felix takes my other hand in his and pulls me towards him, and I let him. Needing to feel him close to me again. "Jenna, no one can blame you for not being ready to be a mom. You're a kid yourself."

"I'm eighteen. So technically not."

He makes a dismissive sound. "Yeah, because everyone gets all their shit together the minute they turn eighteen." He looks into my eyes, his gaze soft. Serious. "You were so young when you had him. You're still so young."

I refrain from pointing out that I'm a year older than him. But I can't refrain from this.

"I'm a shitty person, Felix. It's what I've been for years now, and I'm not good for you or Ty or anyone else." I start pulling away, and he grips my hands tighter. Almost desperately.

"That's not true," he says. "Look, you asked me what I like about you, yeah? What makes me want to date you?"

64

"You don't need to—" I start, but he moves his hands to my upper arms, his fingers light against my skin.

"You're gorgeous, obviously," he says, like that hardly needs saying. "Like incredibly beautiful. And the way you dress is crazy hot."

I don't hate hearing this at all. I *want* him to think these things of me. But right now, it feels like confirmation that maybe that's all I am, even to him.

"But there was more, even before I knew you," he says in a rush, like he can read where my thoughts are going. "You do your own thing, and you give the finger to anyone who disapproves. Often literally." A little smile twitches at his lips. "It's fearless, and I respect that. God, I want to *be* like that sometimes."

I let out a breath. "You are, though. You don't care what your friends think of you dating me, or at least you care little enough that you keep wanting to risk it. You . . . defended me. No one's ever really done that."

"I *don't* care what they think. And as for the defending, I shouldn't get credit for that. That's like basic human decency and I should have been doing it before."

He might be right there. But still. "Yeah, well maybe my 'I don't give a fuck' attitude isn't as brave as you think. Maybe it's all just a front." I hate how my voice quavers a little at the end, proving there's no maybe about it.

Good. He should know that. Especially because it's a truth becoming more and more clear to me the more time I spend with him. If that's what he likes about me, and it's all fake—

"Maybe," he says, like this isn't news to him. Something uncertain flickers in his eyes. "And I do everything I'm told. We all have our masks."

I'm taken aback. Is he saying he doesn't want to . . . what? Get good grades? Date preppy rich girls his parents approve of?

Play the cello?

No, it can't be that. He loves the music too much. I know

65

this, even though I've never heard him say it. I know it because of the way he plays, the emotion that infuses each bow stroke.

I'm about to ask, when he continues on.

"So that was what I liked at first," he says. "But it's so much more, the more I know you. The more you open up to me. You're even more brave, like in this honest, vulnerable way." His hands trail down my sides, his fingers resting at the skin of my waist, sending shivers through the rest of me. "And I feel so comfortable around you, even when I'm kind of freaked out you're going to bail on me."

I tug my lips between my teeth. Comfortable. I wouldn't have thought that word could be sexy, but with him it somehow is. "I might have some idea of how that feels," I say. "The weirdly comfortable. And the freaked out."

He smiles, pressing his forehead to mine again, and it's like the rest of the world—the crowds, the lines, the happy families and the screaming toddlers—all disappear. "I told you before," he says, "that you make me really happy, and I mean it. That isn't something I feel a whole lot. Not really. But with you, I—it's this whole new thing. You don't care about my image or the stuff everyone else sees about me. You actually like *me*. Like somehow you get me as I really am, and you like it. At least, I hope so." There's a teasing quality to this last bit, but a hesitancy in his eyes. Like he really doesn't know for sure.

I put my arms around his waist, and we're close enough now I can feel the heat from his body on my skin. "I really, really do," I murmur. "Even when you drop our baby in my ketchup."

He laughs softly. "And I love your smile, and being the one who makes you smile, and laugh and—"

And even though I want him to go on and on, to hear him say things like this to me forever, I can't resist it anymore. I lean up and kiss him, fiercely. Desperately. Our lips joining and our tongues brushing, and my hands on the back of his neck and his on the small of my back. My heart slamming against my ribs. Because I know now.

I'm in love with him. Fully and completely. I love him and it's so, so wonderful and terrifying, all at the same time.

We pull back, both remembering at the same time, I think, that we're still standing in the middle of Main Street, USA, and probably seconds away from getting kicked out by some hapless Disney employee. But we're breathless, and grinning at each other again.

There's a moment where I almost tell him, but fear keeps the words from forming. Maybe I'm not as brave or vulnerable as he thinks.

But maybe that's something I can get better at.

"Thank you," is what I actually say, an echo of his words to me last night in the car when I curled up against him.

He kisses my forehead, softly. Then he gets a kind of sly smile on his face, and reaches up and squeezes my hair buns again. I laugh and swat at him and then pinch his ass, and then we're both laughing, and chasing each other through the crowds, slowly making our way back to guest services.

When we finally get there, we're both red-cheeked and winded, and you'd think we actually did have sex somewhere out there in the park rather than just running around like little kids at recess.

An employee gives us a raised eyebrow, particularly when we describe our missing robot baby, but then he goes into the back room and comes out with Felix's backpack, from which is emanating a muffled electronic wail. Relief washes over me.

I pull out the baby, who is still wearing Ty's little airplane jammies, and try to soothe it into shutting up. "I wonder how long this thing's been crying for."

"Probably too long for our ninety percent." He jams his hands in his jeans pockets. "Which I guess means I'm going to be keeping my hundred bucks for today."

"You're such an ass, Felix Mays." I bite my lip to keep from grinning.

"Yeah, well, a deal's a deal, Jenna Rollins," he says. "It's good, though. I have to save up for prom. That is, if you ever actually agree to go with me."

There's a giddy flutter in my chest. Him and me, at the prom—something I never thought I'd do, with a guy I never thought would ever really look at me. At least not like this.

"I might," I say. "If you ever actually ask me to."

His brow furrows. "I did. I said I wanted to go to prom with you."

"That's more a declaration of fact than a question, isn't it?"

"Oh my god, *fine*," he says, but he's grinning widely. "Jenna Rollins, will you go to the prom with me?"

"I'm totally in," I say with a smile, not ready yet for him to know that I mean so much more than just the prom.

SEVEN

Felix

After school the next day I convince Jenna to come over to my house. My parents both work until at least dinnertime, and my sister Gabby has classes at UCLA and this part-time job at a bookstore, so I usually have the house to myself.

"If I didn't know better," Jenna says as we head out to my car, "I'd think this was a booty call."

I smile. "Yeah, it might be. Except you still haven't agreed to be my girlfriend."

Jenna smiles back, but she doesn't say anything.

I'm pretty sure she's teasing me, which is fine with me. I may have agreed to have sex with her that first night we went out if she'd consent to be my girlfriend, but if anything I'm more nervous about it now than I was then.

I want to make Jenna happy, more than anything. I want her to feel how much I care about her.

And I'm terrified that if we sleep together, we'll both be disappointed. Her, because I'm not even close to as skilled and experienced as the guys she's been with, and me, because of my own stupid expectations.

I know it's dumb to expect sex to be earth-shattering. I know it was those expectations that made my experience with Julia so disappointing. Sure, being with her felt good, in a way that was marginally more pleasurable than taking care of myself, and I'd heard it takes time to get good at it.

In the five weeks Julia and I lasted after that, I never got any better.

After that, I decided I was being an idiot. I'd bought in to this overinflated idea that sex is some special thing, when really, it's just another means to get yourself off—and ultimately empty and disappointing, kind of like relationships.

But my relationship with Jenna—yes, I'm thinking of it that way, even if she's not technically my girlfriend—is anything but disappointing. I'm amazed, minute to minute, at how spectacular everything feels, like some switch has flipped, and I can now see color after living my entire life in black and white. I meant what I said to her at Disneyland. I never realized how unhappy I was with my life until she came along and made everything new and bright and wonderful.

What if sex . . . isn't? For me, or for her?

"If there's no one at your house in the afternoons," Jenna says, "then you could have been practicing your cello there instead of hogging the music room."

"I could have been. If someone had told me that they needed the space to play. Trust me. There's not usually a lot of competition for that space two hours after school gets out."

I load my cello case into the backseat, and Jenna settles into my car and props her high-heeled boots up on the dashboard, the baby sprawled across her lap. Her skirt rides up her thigh, and I try not to look.

I look anyway, and Jenna smirks at me.

Oh, yeah. She's definitely teasing me. And just because I'm afraid of being with her doesn't mean that I don't want her like crazy.

I shift in my seat, and her smile widens.

Jenna looks out the window as we drive into my neighborhood in Brentwood, up the narrow winding road to the top of the subdivision. Jenna's neighborhood isn't exactly poor—more like lower middle class. The kind of place with little houses with cracked driveways and peeling eaves, but also big shade trees and freshly mowed lawns and flower pots on the porch.

Our house also has a lawn, mowed twice a week by our gardener. My mother has the outside of the house repainted every other year whether the eaves are showing signs of wear or not (and they never are) to keep up with the changing color choices of the home decor gurus she religiously follows.

I want to tell Jenna it doesn't matter that my parents have money and hers don't, but I also don't want to point it out to her, as if doing so would tell her it *should* bother her, even though I know it already does.

"What's your father do?" I ask.

"He's in construction," Jenna answers. "And my mother used to be a teacher, but she quit her job to take care of Ty."

She says it defensively, and I can hear the guilt in her voice.

I decide to change the subject. "Speaking of people who can go home and play, why don't you?"

She shrugs. "I told you I don't like people listening to me play."

Something about that doesn't sit right. If she took lessons when she was younger, her family must have spent a long time listening to her play.

"Are you okay?" I ask.

Jenna looks over at me, and hugs her arms around herself. "Yes. Why?"

I have a hard time putting words to it. Being with Jenna sometimes feels like dating a ghost. She slips in and out of moods, from happy and beaming to sullen and defensive, and I can't always tell what triggers the change.

With someone else, this might have annoyed me, but with Jenna, I just want to be near her, to study her shifting form.

"I have a surprise for you," I say, not answering her question.

"Really? I'm intrigued."

"You should be. It's a good one."

I pull up our long driveway and jump out of the car to open Jenna's door for her. She blinks at me, like she's not sure what to make of that, and I smile, pull my cello case out of the car, and offer her my other hand.

No one else's cars are in the driveway, and I don't see them through the windows in the free-standing garage. I'm glad my parents didn't pick today to decide to come home from work early. It happens every once in a while, after my mom has a hair appointment or my dad had early drinks with his co-workers and took the rest of the afternoon off.

It's not that I don't want Jenna to meet them.

Okay, it is that I don't want Jenna to meet them. They won't approve of her—I already know this. I may not care what neighborhood Jenna lives in, but they will. Julia, whose parents belong to the same country club as mine, barely passed muster to be my girlfriend, because her parents only had a garden pass.

Besides, my mom can be a total bitch, so I'd rather introduce Jenna to the madness that is my home life in layers.

I unlock the front door and let Jenna into the spacious entryway. There aren't any shoes or coats here, only a large rug that my mother had transported from somewhere in Asia, and a leather fainting couch I've never seen either of my parents sit on.

"Wow," Jenna says, looking up at the high vaulted ceiling, like this in and of itself is something to see.

And it is. My mother feels like a house isn't so much a place to live as a showroom to express to your friends how well you're doing. The truth is, my parents haven't been doing as well financially lately, but you wouldn't know it to look at the house. The real estate market may be struggling, but my parents will put every last dime of their retirement accounts into maintaining appearances before they'll let the house show a single sign of wear and tear.

"Come on," I tell Jenna, dropping my backpack but carrying my cello case further into the house. "There's something I want to show you."

Jenna sets the baby down in the entryway and I take her hand and lead her through the house, seeing the immaculate carpets and the ornately-framed paintings as if through Jenna's eyes. God, my parents are pretentious. It's one thing to have money and use it to buy things that make your life better or easier, and it's something else entirely to use it to buy things just to impress people, as if somehow having the money to buy beautiful things is almost as good as being able to make them.

I lead Jenna to the sunroom. The door is closed, because other than me, no one goes in there except when my mom has company. I set my cello case down in the hall. "Okay," I say, spinning around to Jenna. "Close your eyes."

She gives me a suspicious look, and then obliges.

The temptation to kiss her while her eyes are closed is overwhelming. I step in close, wrapping my arms around her. She leans in, her forehead brushing against my chin.

I duck my head and kiss her, pulling her against me and closing my eyes. She doesn't resist, not even a little, and I smile against her lips.

"I knew that's what your surprise was," Jenna says.

"Mmm," I say. "Wrong, Rollins." I open up the door to the sunroom and pull Jenna in. She stumbles forward and opens her eyes.

And stares at my parents' grand piano.

"Whoa," Jenna says. She looks at it for a moment before stepping forward and running her hand gingerly over the polished finish.

Then she looks at me suspiciously. "Does anyone in your family even play?"

"Not really. My dad can, but he never does. And I took lessons when I was eight, but I hated it. Gabby and Dana took lessons, too, and I think Gabby might still be able to play one hand to 'Heart and Soul.' Maybe."

"Oh my god. You have a grand piano that no one ever plays."

"But my mother keeps it in tune," I say. "She has someone

come by every three months. Want to test it?"

Jenna narrows her eyes. "You're trying to get me to play for you."

"I guess I can leave you two alone." I take a step toward the door.

Jenna raises her eyebrows at me, like she's waiting for me to leave.

"Okay, just kidding," I say. "I'm not really going. Unless you require that I sit outside the room and listen, like you've been doing to me."

Jenna turns back to the piano, and runs her black polished nails once over the velvet bench before sliding it carefully out from underneath the piano.

"All right," she says. "You win, you sexy beast."

"I'd appreciate that, if I didn't know you were talking to the piano."

"I am. Hush. Now I'm going to pretend you're not there."

I sit down in the chair I use for practicing. There's no evidence I use this room except for the music stand tucked away in the corner. I play here on Saturdays and in the morning before school, but the carpet has vacuum lines on it. You wouldn't know anyone had been here. I've been erased.

Jenna puts her hands on the keys, and starts to play this haunting song. Her fingers are quick on the keys, and her eyes are downcast, and the sound the piano makes, filling the room with the perfect acoustics that my mom had engineered specially to suit the piano . . . It's the most beautiful sound I've ever heard, in this room or any other.

And then she starts to sing. The song, I quickly realize, is Sarah Bareilles's "Gravity." Jenna's voice is low and rich and sexy as hell, and I'm struck with this need to get up and sit with her, to be close to her. The song itself is pretty, but it's Jenna who's truly beautiful, who fills the whole room with her voice and her presence and this incredible thing that only exists here because she's in it.

Her back is to me, so she can't see me staring, which is probably good, because I know I look like an idiot, but I can't help it. I listen through the first song, and then she picks up another with barely a pause. I've never heard the next one, and it's even more beautiful than the last, a melancholy song about being surrounded by people and yet entirely alone.

She finishes, and the last strains of the music fade before she lowers her hands from the keys. She turns around and looks at me, like she's worried what I think, and I finally let myself move over to sit beside her.

"Damn," I say.

Jenna laughs. "Yeah?"

"Yeah. That second song, did you write that?"

Jenna hesitates, and then nods. "Yeah, that one was mine."

Damn. "Would you play it again?"

Jenna looks uncomfortable. "Why?"

I smile at her. "No reason." But I get up and get my cello case from the hall and open it to pull out my instrument.

Jenna hesitates. "It's harder to pretend you're not here if you play."

I shrug at her, and sit down and run through some warm-ups, making sure my cello is in tune. Jenna watches my hand on the strings, the rise and fall of my bow as I play the scales. I reach the end of the exercise, make a few adjustments, and then run the scales one more time.

Then I look up at her and wait.

"The same song?" Jenna asks. Her voice is quiet, almost reverent.

"Yeah. The last one."

She turns around, and for a moment her fingers pause on the keys, and I think maybe she's not going to do it.

And then she starts to play. I pick up the melody right away, the strong notes of my cello pushing against the beautiful chords from the piano in a way that makes goosebumps rise on my arms. As we hit the chorus I close my eyes and try out a harmony, our music dancing together like experienced partners. I've played with lots of people over the years, even a few duets, but I've never experienced anything like the arousal that comes over me now, not just sexually, although there's definitely that.

It's like every part of my body is awake and aware of her, like the music has stripped us of both our reservations and our clothes, and we're touching each other, holding each other, raw and bare and tender like nothing I've ever felt.

When the song ends, I lower my bow and open my eyes. Jenna keeps looking down at her hands on the keys, her back to me, but I can tell she's breathing as hard as I am.

I get up and lay my cello back in its case. It's a concert-quality instrument and I don't dare lay it anywhere else, but I need it out of my hands. I cross the room, sitting down next to Jenna on the piano bench.

Jenna looks up at me, and there are tears in her eyes. I cup her chin, and I kiss her and kiss her and kiss her. It's more than lust, more than some infatuation. Playing with her like that—it felt like we were speaking to each other's souls. There are all sorts of words I want to put to it, but I'm afraid to, so instead I just hold her and kiss her until she pulls back and buries her face in my neck.

And then I hear a faint noise from the front of the house.

Back in the entryway, the baby is crying.

I'm about to get up, but Jenna beats me to it, hurrying from the room like she's trying to escape, and maybe she is. Or maybe she's just worried about tomorrow's money, since she missed out on today's. The Disneyland escapade reduced us to a seventy-nine percent.

She returns with the baby on her shoulder, her face flushed. I scoot over, indicating to the space beside me on the piano bench, and she joins me, looking up at the thick suede curtains. They're ornate enough that they ought to be gaudy, but they work so well with the room that they aren't. I'll give this to my mom: if she's going to buy a bunch of stuff just to show off, at least she knows how to do it right.

"Your parents aren't going to like me, are they?" Jenna asks.

I press my lips together, and decide to tell her the truth. "No.

But I don't care what they think."

Jenna turns and looks at me, like she doesn't quite believe me, and I shake my head. "My parents disapprove of everything," I say. "It won't be new to them."

That's not exactly true. My parents do disapprove of many things, but they very much approve of my dedication to my grades, to my music, to my future studies at Juilliard, which they long ago deemed the only acceptable school for their musical genius son. Everything I've done over the last several years has been aimed at getting me there, because the truth is I'm not a genius. I just love the music, and I work harder than anyone else.

It's exhausting, I realize. I never noticed how tired it made me before I had something else to compare it to.

"I'm not worth this," Jenna says. "All the sacrifices you're making for me."

I laugh, and Jenna looks alarmed. "Yes," I say. "The sacrifices. Having to hang out with a beautiful girl who I'm crazy about, who's going to let me take her to prom, and who I'm still hoping one of these days is going to agree to be my girlfriend."

"You really want that."

I nod. "Of course I do. Being with you—it's incredible." I lace her fingers in with mine. "My life was so hollow, and I didn't even realize it until I met you and it wasn't anymore."

Jenna blinks, and I think for a second maybe she's going to cry. "My parents sold our piano," she says.

I squint at her. "What?"

"That's why I don't play at home. My dad got laid off and money was tight and they needed to pay bills, so they sold our piano. I don't have one at home anymore."

I look over our grand piano that no one ever plays. "You're welcome to play this one, any time you want."

"Any time your parents aren't here."

"No," I say. "Even then. Your music is so beautiful, I think that's one thing even they won't be able to complain about."

Jenna smiles, like this is the first time I've told her I like her music, and she takes my hand.

"Yes," she says.

"Yes, you'll play here?"

"Yes, I'll be your girlfriend." She turns into me, and raises her hand to brush my cheek.

"Awesome," I say, and Jenna laughs, and then her mouth meets mine.

I've never been happier in my life.

EIGHT

Jenna

Felix drives me home at around five-thirty, before his parents get home from work. He doesn't make a big deal about it, but from the way he kept glancing at the clock in between alternating bouts of making out and talking on the floor of the sunroom, it was clear he was keeping a close eye on the time.

I get it. I already knew his parents would hate me, and that was before I stepped foot in his house/mansion. It wasn't just the stark wealth difference, though. It was how immaculate everything was, how perfectly tailored and crisply maintained. Nobody wants their son dating me, but especially not the kind of people who need to live in that kind of magazine photo-shoot-level perfection.

It should make me feel bad for me, but really it makes me feel bad for Felix. That's some hardcore pressure right there, and I think I might be starting to understand what he meant about the masks he wears.

I want to understand even more. I want to know everything about him, which is weird for me. Usually, I feel like the less I get to know people, the better. Better for them, and better for me, because it's bound to lead to disappointment either way.

Felix, as usual, appears to be an exception. He's my *boyfriend* now. It doesn't get much more exceptional than *that*.

Said boyfriend also has his hand on my leg as he drives, right where my skirt ends, so that a couple of his fingers are on my skirt and a couple are on the skin just beneath, and it's driving me a little insane to not tackle him right now, even though that would lead to a major car accident.

He's telling me a story about some stupid stunt some friends of his pulled on their orchestra teacher, but his fingers inch just the slightest bit higher, under the hem of my skirt, and my breath catches like he's touching a lot more than just my upper thigh. It's kind of crazy the effect this guy has on me. How heightened every touch is.

His smile turns mischievous. "Sorry. Am I distracting you?" I'm not the only one who likes to tease, apparently.

"A *little*," I say, emphasizing that word he likes so much and shooting him my own devilish look. "If you want to really distract me, we could always pull over."

"Sex on the side of the road. I'm starting to think you have a thing for that."

"Maybe I just have a thing for *you*."

"I'm definitely not complaining about that." He tickles my leg with a twitch of his fingers, but doesn't move them up any higher, so I'm thinking roadside sex is a no-go.

Which, honestly, I'm happy about. I don't want our first time to be some cramped quickie in the Denny's parking lot two blocks from my house. I want it to be *special*, even though I can only imagine the look Ian would give me if he heard me say that. Being with Felix is going to mean something, though, I know it.

What I don't know is when it'll actually happen. I'm his girlfriend now, but it's not like the minute I said yes, he scooped me up and carried me off to his bedroom. In fact, our make-out didn't even go as far as it did in the car that first night—at least in that I kept my shirt on, though his hands definitely found their way underneath—so he must be waiting for something more than just the girlfriend thing.

And as much as I want to be with him like that, I'm okay waiting until he's ready. The making-out alone is better than any sex I've ever had, so it's not like I'm not getting plenty from where we're at now.

"So you weren't going to join your friends in this daring clarinet heist?" I ask, bringing it back to the story.

"No way," he says, grinning. "Because even I, the ultimate orchestra nerd, know that anything that can be described as a 'clarinet heist' is super lame. And besides, it was going to cut into my practice time."

"Which I think I've been doing quite a bit this week."

He shrugs, his eyes cutting over to me. "*You're* worth it."

Giddy warmth pulses in me, as it does whenever he says something like that. About how I'm worth being with, how much he wants to date me and doesn't care what others think or say or do about it.

Still, I don't want to deprive him of his music time, which I know he loves. "Well, since I'm not dragging you to Anaheim tonight, hopefully you'll have time to catch—oh shit."

That last bit because we've just pulled onto my street, and there in the front yard is my mom, planting some yellow pansies, and Rachel, playing a game of chase with Ty.

So much for me sneaking in without having to see any of them.

And even worse, there's no way my mom won't see that I'm being dropped off by Felix—who she will undoubtedly have heard all about from Rachel.

Felix glances over at me, looking a little confused, which is warranted, given that he knows Rachel and has met Ty. But my parents . . . It's not that they won't like him—pretty much the opposite, I think. I'm just not sure I'm ready to deal with the shock they'll have about what a guy like him is doing with *me*.

I don't know if Rachel's convinced them I'm dating him just to spite her.

We pull into the driveway, and both Rachel and Mom look

over. Ty is too busy poking at something in the grass to notice.

"If you don't want me to meet your mom," Felix starts, but I shake my head.

"Nah, it's okay. Just . . . god, I'd say be prepared, but I don't even know what to prepare for. They'll like you. They just might be freaks about it."

He grins and squeezes my leg. "I'm pretty good with parents."

At least one of us is.

"Feel free to run at any time," I say, as he puts the car in park.

"Not a chance."

There's that fluttery feeling in my chest again; how does he manage to make me feel so good?

I open the car door to get out and hear him doing the same on the other side. My mom stands up, brushing dirt from her gardening gloves, and even Ty finally looks up from whatever bug or interesting leaf he'd been inspecting. Rachel gives an awkward little wave at Felix, and a stab of guilt hits me. She'd be so upset if she knew I'd told him about her crush. Not to mention the story about her throwing up with excitement for the Dumbo ride.

"Hey Rachel," Felix says. If he's feeling weird knowing about her being into him, he doesn't show it. "Hey Ty."

Ty bounds over to him as if he's known Felix forever, and holds out his little chubby hand, on which a bug curls into a tight ball. "Look! I have ro-wee po-wee!"

Felix laughs. "Yeah, that's a pretty big roly-poly you got there, kid. Nice."

Ty beams up at him, and then pokes at the rolled-up bug, pushing him around on his palm.

"Hello, you two," my mom says, walking forward, her eyes bright and wider than usual. "It looks like I'm the only one who hasn't met your friend yet, Jenna."

I hold back a grimace. "Mom, this is Felix Mays. He's my, um. My boyfriend."

Now my mom's eyes practically bug out of her head. With

82

Rachel's chestnut brown hair, my gray eyes, and a young face, my mom's an attractive woman. But even she can't pull off *that* look well.

I try not to notice how Rachel's expression darkens.

"It's nice to meet you, Mrs. Rollins," Felix says smoothly, extending his hand.

My mom blinks at it for a moment, and then shakes his hand. "Wow. This is quite a surprise. I mean, a nice surprise. To meet you. I've heard great things about you, Felix."

Rachel looks away, and that guilt slices me again. It wasn't from *me* that Mom heard anything about Felix.

"I'm glad to hear that," Felix says. "I've been looking forward to meeting you guys."

I want to shoot him a challenging look, like *Really? Have you?*

"What a polite young man!" my mom says. "Ty, why don't you go inside and get Pops? He needs to meet Felix. Or—do you want to come inside? I'm sure we have some snacks. Maybe pie. Do you like pie, Felix?"

Oh my god, is my mom fangirling my boyfriend? This is even worse than I'd feared.

"I—yeah, pie's great." Even Felix sounds a little taken aback by the cheery onslaught, but he covers it well.

"My dad used to make great pies, especially blueberry," my mom continues, walking toward the house. "He and Jenna used to bake together all the time, whenever they'd come out to visit. Do you remember that, Jenna? You loved making pies."

I do remember, and she's right. Some of my favorite childhood memories come from baking with my grandpa. But my cheeks burn anyway. Not because I'm embarrassed for Felix to know this about me, but because it's so obvious how much my mom longs for me to be that little kid again. How much she wants to pretend the person I am now doesn't really exist.

And most days, I can't say I blame her.

"She was so good at it, too," my mom says as she opens the front door.

"I bet she was." Felix gives me a side smile.

For some reason, this makes me think of how impressed he was—he, Felix Mays!—with my piano-playing, with my song. The look on his face when I'd turned around, like he was witnessing something so beautiful it was damn near miraculous—which is probably how I look listening to him play.

And playing together, oh my god.

I can't resist reaching out and grabbing his hand. Even if that's only bound to encourage my mom in her weirdness.

We go in the house, and Ty darts by us towards the Christmas tree. I'm pretty sure it has become a year-round tree given how much he loves yelling "Doom! Doom!" It's a good thing Mom traded out the glass ball ornaments for more toddler-friendly paper-mache ones that Ty can strip the tree of every day.

Honestly, I kind of like still having it up. It's the first year we've had a Christmas tree at all since before Ty was born, since my mom spent the last few years as a Jehovah's Witness. That didn't stick any more than her previous attempts at finding religion, so now we get our tree back, and it's like we're making up for lost holiday time.

"Daryl," my mom calls, and my dad walks out from the kitchen, a bottle of Snapple in hand. He's obsessed with the stuff. He's a tall man—unlike the rest of my family, for whom "petite" is a fairly generous description—with thinning dark blond hair and a thickening belly, though his arms are pretty muscular from construction work.

"Hi there," Dad says. He looks between me and Rachel, trying to figure out which one Felix belongs to and clearly coming up confused either way.

"Hi, Mr. Rollins," Felix says, extending his hand again like he did for Mom. "I'm Felix." Dad shakes it.

"Fee-yix!" Ty shouts happily, swinging his plastic sword to knock another ornament free. "Fee-yix, look!"

"I see it, kid. That's awesome." Felix looks like he does indeed think Ty's game is pretty awesome, and it makes me

84

smile despite the fact that I'm standing in the midst of my entire family. With my boyfriend.

"Felix is Jenna's boyfriend," my mom says, with no small amount of significance. I'm not sure if Dad is picking up the exact mental vibes she's sending him, if he's heard of Felix before like mom obviously has, but his eyebrows shoot up in surprise.

"Really." He looks at me almost suspiciously. Like he thinks this is some game I'm playing just to mess with them—Jenna claiming this nice, well-mannered boy in the button-down shirt is her boyfriend! I feel my palm sweat against Felix's.

"Really," I say, though I know it comes out sounding cold.

I can't seem to help it; that's the way it pretty much always comes out when I'm talking to them.

"Well, it's nice to meet you," Dad says, after looking at me for a beat. "Come on in, sit down." He gestures to the living room where Ty whacks another Orb of Evil.

"Do we really have to—" I start, but Mom cuts me off.

"So Felix, tell us about yourself." She sits on the couch and Dad sits in his armchair.

Felix gives me a quick questioning look, like making sure I'm okay with this whole "parents getting to the know the boyfriend" thing, and I give a little nod back, because it's happening no matter what I think.

So we go sit down on the couch by my mom. Rachel sort of hovers in the space between the kitchen and living room, not looking at anyone.

"Well," Felix starts. "I'm a junior, and I'm in Jenna's health class. We were partnered up for a project, and that's how we got to know each other."

Uh-oh. We left the baby in the car. Probably for the best, as I can't imagine adding our robot progeny to this situation would lessen the awkwardness. Hopefully whatever my parents intend to do here—some cheesy "don't hurt my daughter" routine? Throw him a celebratory "thank god she's dating someone her own age" parade?—won't take too long.

I notice Felix doesn't say that our "getting to know each other" started just two days ago and was jogged along by me propositioning him several times in his car. Though all of that would likely be far less surprising to my parents than the whole boyfriend thing.

"You're in a class with Rachel, too, is that right?" my mom asks, and both Rachel and I glare at her.

Felix pretends not to notice. "Yeah, that's right. Honors English." He gives a little smile to Rachel, who smiles back, though with pink cheeks. "And I play the cello," Felix continues. "I have since I was ten. I want to play professionally someday."

"Really, a musician?" Dad perks up at this. He's the one who taught me to play piano, though I surpassed him years ago.

"He's really incredible," I say, and both my parents look at me in surprise, like they kind of forgot I was even here.

Felix squeezes my hand. "So is Jenna."

"You've heard her play?" Mom's eyes dart back and forth between us. "Jenna, I didn't know you played anymore."

I hold in a wince. Part of the reason they sold the piano was my fault, I suppose. I began avoiding my family so much that the only times I ever played was when no one was home. So it made sense, given how many aspects of my life I've tossed out in favor of parties and teenage pregnancy and ennui, that they would assume my musical inclinations went out with the rest of it. If I'd told them otherwise, they probably would have kept it, tried to find some other way to get the money. But the reason they needed it in the first place was really my fault, and I knew it, so I kept my mouth shut.

I shrug. "Sometimes."

There's a heavy beat of silence, and I feel myself folding inward.

It shouldn't be this hard. My parents are good people, like my sister. Friendly and kind. They love me, no matter how much they hate the things I do, the hurt I cause them, the way I screw up their lives.

And maybe that's the problem. I know what I've done to them, and what I continue doing to them by not even trying to be the daughter they wish I was. And I can't help but worry that Felix will see this and wonder, like the rest of them, like I do sometimes, why the hell I just *can't*.

"And your parents? What do they do?" My mom asks, breaking the silence. "And where do you live?"

"My dad is an accountant for film companies and my mom is in real estate," Felix says. There's a tiny pause before he adds, "We live in Brentwood."

"Is that so?" Mom smooths out her jeans, as if just now realizing they aren't designer slacks of some kind. "Very impressive." She gives a nervous smile. "And what do they think of you two dating?"

My chest squeezes tighter.

Felix flicks a glance at me. "We, um, haven't told them yet. It's pretty new."

"Of course," Mom says, nodding a little too emphatically, and I want to crawl in a hole and die. It sucks bad enough being the kind of girl Felix is justifiably afraid to introduce to his parents. The kind of girl his parents would in no way think is good enough for him. It sucks even worse knowing my own parents would agree with them.

"Oh!" Mom says, jumping up. "I said I'd get you pie."

Ty perks up at this. "Pie! I want pie, pease."

"I'll get you some, too, sweetie. Daryl?"

"Sure thing." Dad leans back in the armchair and pops open his Snapple. "So, Felix. Smart honors student, cellist, professional future ambitions . . ." He lets out a chuckle. "You sure you picked the right daughter?"

My stomach lurches, and Felix's parent-schmoozing smile drops.

"Daryl!" My mom says, at the same time Rachel yells, "Dad!"

I don't say anything.

"What? I was just . . . it's a joke," Dad says, wilting visibly. I feel kind of bad for him. I don't think he really meant anything mean by it. He looks at me. "Jen, honey, you know it was just a joke."

I do. It's one of those jokes that's funny because it's true, and we all know it.

"Daryl, why don't you come help me in the kitchen," my mom says through clenched teeth, and Dad gets up to join her, his shoulders slumped.

Felix's mouth works soundlessly for a beat. "Jenna," he says quietly, but Ty grabs his hand.

"Fee-yix! Come fight da tree with me."

Felix looks at me, torn, and I smile. "It's cool. If you want to. He'd love it."

Ty drags Felix over to the tree, and I notice the angry look Rachel is giving me when Felix isn't looking. She makes a gesture towards upstairs, and I know she wants to talk to me. I'm tempted to just pretend I don't know what she means, or even give her the patented Jenna Rollins one-finger reply, but honestly, I'm going to hear it eventually. Might as well deal with the whole family shit-storm at once.

"I'm going to run upstairs for a minute, is that okay?" I ask Felix, who is being handed the sword by Ty—quite the honor, actually. Ty rarely lets anyone else touch the thing. "If you want to go, you can. It's really okay if you don't want to deal with all this and—"

"I'm fine," Felix says. "Besides, it's not every day I get to fight Orbs of Evil on the Christmas Tree of Doom."

I smile, but I still feel like my gut is all twisted up inside. "Yeah, well. I'll play piano at your house, and you fight holiday evil at mine. Feels like an even trade."

Then I head upstairs, just behind Rachel. She leads me into her room, which is decidedly cleaner and less covered in piles of black clothing than mine. Books all over the place, though. Pictures of her smiling with Ty, and with my parents, and with her nice, normal, well-adjusted friends. Awards on the wall.

You sure you picked the right daughter?

88

"What do you want?" I ask wearily.

"He's your boyfriend now," she says, glaring at me.

"Was there a question in there? Yes, he is."

"Seriously, Jenna, don't do this to him. It's mean and it sucks."

I should get an award for not replying that he likes the sucking part. But I still feel bad about having told Felix about Rachel's crush, so I try to blunt my natural bitchiness. "I'm not doing anything mean to him, Rachel. I know you think I'm messing with him, or you, but I'm not."

"Really," she says. "So you're really going to be his girlfriend and not sleep around with other guys?"

"Yes. I really am." That part wasn't even something I had to think twice about. I don't want other guys. I want Felix.

I'm in love with Felix.

The thought still catches my breath, even with a whole day to think about little else.

"Sure," she says, like she doesn't believe it for a minute. "And what about Ty?"

"What about him? Felix knows I have a kid. He's down there playing Tree of Doom with him right now."

"Exactly. And when you break up with Felix because you're bored or whatever, then Ty loses him, too. You get that, right? You bring people over and Ty gets attached and—"

"Is this really about Ty? Or are you worried about that yourself?"

"I think the only one just thinking about themselves is you."

We glare at each other, even as the guilt makes knot upon knot in me.

Finally, I close my eyes, let out a breath. "Look, Rachel. I know you think I'm doing this *at* you. That I'm only with him because you liked him, to piss you off. But I'm not." I open my eyes to see her watching me warily. And maybe it's the influence of being more open with Felix than I am with anyone, ever, but I find myself wanting her to know the truth. "I liked him for a long time. I liked him before I had any idea that you did, too. And now I think I lo—" My voice catches. *Love him*, I almost said.

But I can't bring myself to say it out loud yet. Not to Felix, and not to her.

She stares at me, and I know she gets what I was about to say. "Oh," she says quietly. She drops her gaze to the carpet.

"Yeah."

"Does he . . . too?"

I chew my lip. "I don't know. He really likes me, I know that. He cares about me in a way that—" I shake my head, not even sure myself how to end that. "But it's only been a few days. I don't expect him to feel that way yet. Maybe someday. I mean, I don't think most guys sit around and think about whether they're in love, you know?"

Rachel gets a strange look on her face, totally at odds with the surprise or hurt I assume she's feeling. It's more like . . . guilt.

"What?" I demand.

"It's not really anything," she says quickly. "I just—I heard Angela Harwick talking to one of her friends."

I wrinkle my nose reflexively. Angela is one of Felix's orchestra girl fan club, who's probably spent the better part of the year trying to angle her way into Julia's vacated spot.

"About me?"

Rachel purses her lips. "Sort of, I guess. I mean, everyone's talking about you and Felix, and I'm sure that's why she was talking about this. About him and Julia."

A little drip of ice slides along my spine. Not because I think there's anything going on with Julia. But I can tell from the look on Rachel's face that whatever she heard isn't going to be something I'll like.

I don't say anything, just wait for Rachel to continue, and after a long beat, she does.

"Angela said he was so in love with Julia. Like, he told her that. And then they slept together, and Julia says it wasn't long after that he stopped answering her calls, or paying much attention to her. He just started kind of ignoring her, but he wouldn't tell her why. Angela said she was so hurt and heartbroken, and she broke up with him, hoping he'd realize he missed her and wanted her back, but he never did."

My mouth has dropped open, and I snap it shut, trying to process this. First off, I'm not sure Angela's recounting is unbiased journalism, but in a general sense, it squares with several rumors I heard around that time.

Was he really in love with *Julia*? He's not the kind of guy who would say that just to get a girl to sleep with him, like the story implies—though I suppose he could have been, and realized later what a dick thing that was to do. But it's hard for me to imagine that being the case, given how much sex he could have had with me by now had that been his primary goal in life.

Or did he just think he was in love with her, and realize at some point that she's actually super annoying and shallow as a cookie sheet?

It happens, I suppose. I'd thought I was in love once, for like a nanosecond. Back when I was fourteen, and a cute sixteen-year-old guy I met at the mall invited me to my first party. It was a night of a lot of firsts—my first beer, my first real make-out session. My first time having sex. The whole night was like a blur, even then, moving faster than I could keep up, but I believed it meant something. Not just the sex, but all of it. I believed it meant I was becoming this new person, changing from the quiet, unsure girl who was sad a lot for no reason into this dynamic, fun girl who someone wanted—maybe even loved.

I was so, so wrong. That guy never contacted me again, wouldn't return my texts or calls. I saw him a few times at parties later, when I was going because I'd discovered that alcohol and guys were at least good for numbing the pain, or making me forget it for a little while, but he didn't say anything then, either. He once drunkenly hit on me like he'd never met me before, and I told him to go fuck himself—even party Jenna has some standards.

91

I was right about one thing, though. I definitely became a new person. I never again was stupid enough to believe that a quick fuck in a guest bedroom at a party means anything, no matter what the guy says about how he's falling for me.

I never again was stupid enough to believe a lot of things.

Felix makes me want to believe in some of them again—that a guy like him could really care about me. That maybe one day I could have the love story too. I know that whatever I felt for that guy, years ago, was nothing compared to what I feel for Felix. A match flame compared to a raging bonfire.

My knotted gut tightens and tightens.

Is that why he hasn't wanted to sleep with me yet, even though I'm his girlfriend? Does he want to be in love, like he was with Julia?

What if he changes his mind about me too?

"I'm sorry," Rachel says. "It probably doesn't mean anything, you know? I still think Felix is a really good guy. But I thought—I don't know, if you really care about him, it seemed like you should know."

It's not lost on me, even in my newfound anxiety, that somehow Rachel has switched from trying to protect Felix to trying to protect me.

"Thanks," I say quietly.

She scuffs the carpet with her toe. "Dad shouldn't have said that, about the right daughter thing."

"Yeah, probably not. It kind of sucked for both of us, huh?"

She gives a humorless laugh. "Yeah, well, that's Dad. He gets a little Snapple in him and can't keep his mouth shut." She shrugs. "Anyway, yeah, I have a crush on Felix. But it's not like a big deal. I also have crushes on two guys in my PE class. Just don't go dating them, okay?"

I let out a small laugh, too. "Trust me, I won't."

In a movie, it feels like this would be a hugging moment, but Rachel and I haven't hugged in years. So we just look at each other awkwardly, and then I turn around and head downstairs, visions of Felix confessing his undying love to Julia in my head, along with visions of him suddenly realizing the mistake he's made with me. Avoiding me, afraid to look me in the eyes and just tell me he doesn't want me anymore.

I force myself to shove all these thoughts out of my head. They won't do anyone any good.

I get back downstairs and hear Ty giggling his happiest giggle. Felix is holding up the ornaments and just as Ty swings for them, he bobs them up higher, so Ty's swing goes wide.

"Oh no!" Felix says, a huge grin on his face. "These Orbs keep jumping. They are so evil."

Ty laughs again. "Evil orbs! Stop jumping, orbs!"

It's crazy adorable, seeing them play together, and it makes me anxious as all hell for some reason, even as it melts me a bit inside.

There are a few plates of pie sitting out on the coffee table, and Mom is watching Felix and Ty play like she can't believe what she's seeing. She blinks when I enter the room. "Jenna! I was just telling Felix that he should stay for dinner."

Felix looks over at me, his eyebrows raised.

He would, I think, but I don't know that I can handle any more of my dad's jokes, or my mom's barely restrained glee.

"Felix and I were going out to dinner," I say. "And we should probably take off now, yeah?"

Felix barely hesitates. "Yeah, that's probably good. Thanks for the game, kid." He ruffles Ty's blond hair. I melt a little more.

My mom makes protesting noises, but I manage to get Felix out of the house and back into his car before she can plot some way to force feed him chicken casserole.

"So I'm taking you to dinner?" he asks.

"You don't have to." I feel a little idiotic for dragging him out so suddenly. "I just needed to get out of there. But if you need to go home and practice, that's cool. I can just hang out somewhere and walk home later." I hope he can't tell how much I want him to stay with me, even just a little longer.

Felix watches me for a few seconds, and then takes my hand again. "Okay, maybe I mis-phrased the question," he says. "*Where* am I taking you to dinner?"

I grin over at him, that happy flutter back. "I picked Disneyland. This one's on you."

NINE

Felix

I briefly consider taking Jenna somewhere extravagant for dinner, but decide against it. This relationship has been hell on my bank account, and I really do need some money left for prom.

Plus, aside from paying her to do our homework, it's not like I need to spend a lot of money. The Disneyland thing was basically a dare. She doesn't expect things like that.

Which might be the problem, because it makes them a lot more fun.

I drive to my favorite burger place. "This okay?" I ask.

"Yeah, great," Jenna says.

She doesn't sound like it's great, even though she seemed happy enough about actually going out to dinner. But I don't think it has anything to do with my choice of restaurants. Something's bothering her, which I figured was the case when she announced we were going to dinner after I was supposed to be dropping her off at home. I'm missing practice again today, but I don't mind. My private teacher—who's also a music professor at UCLA—would be pissed if he knew, but All-State and honors philharmonic are both over for the season, and it's not like I actually have to try that hard to play the pieces for the school orchestra final concert.

I can't blow it off forever, but two days in a row aren't going to kill me.

Which was not something I would have guessed I'd be saying at the beginning of the week.

"Are you upset about what your dad said?" I ask. "Because that was out of line. And yes, I'm sure I'm with the right daughter. That isn't even a thing."

"I know," Jenna says. "It's fine."

But it isn't fine, and the less she talks about it, the more worried I am. I try to come around to open her door, but she gets out before I can reach her. I grab our baby from the back seat and bring it in. Hopefully she won't make too much noise in the restaurant and get us kicked out. I imagine they're less tolerant about robot babies than real ones.

It's Wednesday night, and the place isn't terribly busy. We're seated at a booth in the back, and I'm a little worried when she sits across from me instead of next to me. I put the baby on my lap and pat it absently.

"Did I do something wrong?" I ask.

She shakes her head, but doesn't say anything. I'm wondering if maybe I shouldn't have come in to meet her family, or shouldn't have been so friendly with her kid. I met him before, but that was, well, *before*. Before I knew she was into me, before we were together, before I started feeling things I'm afraid to name.

Meeting him again was a wakeup call. I'm dating a girl with a kid, and as deep as I'm in this with her, that has to have implications for the future. A future we haven't talked about. A future in which I have no idea what she wants.

"How did it go with Rachel?" I ask her.

"Okay, actually." She flips through the menu, not looking up at me. "She gave me a big lecture about how I shouldn't do this to you, because you're such a good guy. And then I told her that I actually like you, and she was shocked. Apparently I'm not allowed to have feelings. Or be interested in guys for more than just sex."

My breath catches. That's more stuff we haven't talked about. We're together, now, and that's what I said my line was for sleeping together, but obviously we haven't done that yet and I'm not sure when we will.

There are so many things I want to talk about right now, and all of them are loaded.

"So, what's the situation with Ty?" I ask. "He calls you Mom. When you're older, will he live with you, or will he stay with your parents?"

Jenna is quiet for a long minute. "I don't know."

I nod. "That makes sense. It's a lot to take on, yeah?"

She shrugs, and I can't stand it anymore. I reach across the table to take her hand.

She looks up at me, like this startles her.

"Hey, it's cool," I say. "I'm not judging you. I just want to understand what's happening."

Jenna's expression softens. "The truth is, I really have no idea. I've never told my parents that I want to take care of him. And they've never said anything about it, either. I think they don't want me to move out and take him with me if I'm going to keep going to parties and coming home drunk, but I would never do that." She's quiet for another moment. "I just don't know if I could ever be a real mom to him. To take care of him like he deserves."

I nod. "You're still really young, though. You could grow into it, if you want to."

Jenna shakes her head. "I don't think it works that way."

There's a sadness in her voice, and a fear. I close my other hand around hers. "But you want it to."

She hesitates for a long moment, and then she nods.

I meant it when I said I wouldn't judge her decision. She had a baby when she was fifteen. If her parents had basically adopted the kid and that's how it was, I'd get that.

But the fact that she wants to be his mom, and had him so young that she hasn't been able to . . . I hurt for her, and for her parents, and for the entire situation.

"Does that scare you?" Jenna asks.

I shake my head before I fully think about it, and Jenna gives me a look.

"Really? It doesn't scare you to be dating someone with a kid who's three years old when you're seventeen."

"Okay," I say. "It's a lot to think about. But it doesn't scare me *off*."

Jenna falls quiet again, and just as I'm about to ask her again what's going on, the waitress shows up to take our order. We both order burgers and fries and when she walks away again, Jenna pulls her hand away from mine.

"Don't ever tell me you love me unless you mean it," she says.

My mouth falls open as I try to make sense of this statement. "Um, okay."

Jenna bites her lip, like she didn't mean to say that, but clearly she's been stewing on it for a while. "Rachel may have heard something from Julia's friend Angela."

Oh. I understand now, but I let her finish, because I want to know exactly what she heard.

"Angela said you told Julia you were so in love with her, and then after you guys had sex, you didn't care about her anymore. Like you just said that to get her to sleep with you."

"I didn't," I say. "That's not what happened."

"Okay. Then what happened?"

She sounds like she's reserving judgment, and I don't know whether to be grateful for that or terrified. "I dated Julia for a while. And she was cute and we had fun, and I really wanted to be in love with her."

"But you weren't," Jenna says.

"No, I wasn't. But I thought I was when I said that. And I don't know that I said I was *so* in love with her, but I did say I love you, and then we had sex, and I rapidly figured out that it was hormones, not love."

Jenna shrinks back on the bench, like maybe this disgusts

her. She'd be right to feel that way.

"I know," I say "It was a shitty thing to do. But it wasn't intentional."

"Did you tell her that?" Jenna asks.

"No. I kind of . . . neglected her until she broke up with me."

"Angela apparently said she broke up with you hoping you'd stop taking her for granted and come begging her to take you back."

"Oh, god, is that what she wanted?" I cringe. The bad part is, I can see it. "Well that's not what happened. If anything, I was relieved."

"She probably still wants you back," Jenna says.

"If you're floating that to find out if it's a temptation, it's not. I don't want to get back together with Julia. I want to be with you."

Jenna straightens. "Just don't tell me you love me unless you're sure."

I'm sure, I want to say. The corners of my eyes start to burn, and I consider the impulse.

Am I in love with Jenna?

The way I feel about her is so deep, so visceral, so involuntary that it's hard for me to put words to it. I want her with this hunger that feels desperate and insatiable. There are reasons I can't be with her twenty-four hours a day, but every part of me wishes I could. I'm more physically attracted to her than I ever was with Julia, but it's so much more than that.

I can sit with her like this and not be fixated on the next time we can be alone and make out. I think about her when we're not together, not just to fantasize about sex, but about just being with her. And even though it's only been a few days, I want to talk about the future. I want to picture my future with her in it, even if it means that future doesn't include Juilliard, or anything my parents have planned for me.

Right now, I can't picture myself going to New York, but I don't know if I can fully picture myself staying, either. My future, which has always looked like a train track, now feels like the open sea. I could go anywhere. Be anything.

There are two things I want: to be with Jenna, and to play cello. If I could have those two things, I know I could be happy. I've been wrong before, but this time . . .

I'm in love with Jenna. I want to tell her, but she's just told me not to.

God, after what I did with Julia, will she ever be able to believe me?

"Okay," I say. "I won't say it unless I'm sure."

"Good." She looks down at the table, and the way I feel about her sits in my chest like a stone. Maybe I can't tell her the whole truth, but I have to tell her something or I'm going to burst.

"I'm more serious about you already than I ever was about her," I say. "And if you want to take steps to see if you can get comfortable being Ty's mom, I'm all for it."

"Really?"

"Yeah, of course. We could do things with him together, if you wanted. I mean, if your parents are okay with it. We could start small. Take him to the park, or something. Try not to forget him on the swing set."

Jenna smiles. "Yeah, maybe."

She still looks sad, and I wish I knew how to fix it. I wish I knew how to make up for any of the countless things I'm doing wrong.

"You still want this, right?" I ask her.

"This? You mean, us?"

"Yeah. You're being quiet, and I'm a little afraid this is about to be the world's shortest relationship." More than a *little* afraid. The thought guts me.

Jenna shakes her head. "I definitely still want this. I'm sorry. I should have let you go home and practice. And you have homework, right? I didn't mean to keep you here like this."

"Jenna," I say. "You're not keeping me here. I *want* to be with you. God, all the time, I want to be with you. If I could

100

just follow you around all day, every day, I would."

I'm worried that's a little strong, but Jenna gives me the first warm, genuine smile I've seen since before we arrived at her house.

I love you, I think, feeling those words in every part of me. *I love you.*

I want to honor her request to be sure before I tell her, and I don't know how I could ever be more sure than I am right now, but she has no reason to believe me. I've been wrong before.

Our food arrives, and we dig in. I think we both kind of forgot to eat for most of the day, and have been subsisting on kisses and adrenaline. Our knees press together under the table, and I reach down and rub the inside of her thigh with one hand.

God, I want to make love to her. And I suppose confessing that I'm *in* love with her wasn't a requirement for being with her, unless things have changed. Still, announcing over hamburgers that I want to have sex with her seems about as romantic as having sex by the side of the road.

And speaking of unsexy conversations—

"I was thinking," I say, clearing my throat. "I was thinking maybe we should get tested."

Jenna rolls her eyes. "I can. You don't need to."

"I've had sex."

"Yeah, but only with Julia. And she was a virgin, too, yeah?"

"Yeah," I say. "But I can still get tested. I want to."

"You don't have to do that just to make yourself feel better. I get why you want me to. I actually get tested every couple of months, but I've had sex since the last time, so I can do it again."

"And I will, too," I say. "I insist."

Jenna gives me a look like I'm patronizing her, but I just shrug. I don't want to make her feel bad about her past. It doesn't bother me in a jealous way, though I do have the general urge to burn down all the college party houses in the greater Los Angeles area whenever I think too hard about it.

"So you want to wait until we get results," Jenna says. "So

you can be sure not to catch anything."

Oh, god. That's not what I meant. "No," I tell her. "It's not that. We'd need to use protection anyway, so it's not really a big deal."

Jenna gives me a look like she isn't sure this is true, and I curse myself for messing this up all over again.

"I'm mostly worried about you," I say. "That's all."

She picks at her burger bun. "You shouldn't have to worry. You should be with someone who hasn't slept with who even knows how many guys."

I reach for her hand under the table, but she pulls it away.

"Jenna," I say, "I don't care about that. Really, I don't."

She glares at me, and her voice gets increasingly angry as she speaks. "It doesn't bother you that I go to parties and get wasted as fast as I can, that I'll take any pill I'm handed, that I'll do anything that any guy wants to do to me, or wants me to do to him, that I black out and I don't even know how many guys I've been with, or what they've done."

A deep rage simmers in my chest, a primal desire to have been there for her, to have protected her from that. The fact that she's been treated this way for years, most of it when she was underage—

"It bothers me," I say. "I hate that this happened to you."

"It didn't *happen* to me." Her voice gets louder, and she pulls her knees away from mine, so we're not touching at all. "I *did* that. I was at parties like that *last weekend*. I could probably count the number of guys I've been with in the last *week* on more than one hand, if I remembered enough to count them at all."

"I know!" I say, too loud, and a few heads in the restaurant turn. I flush, lowering my voice. "I know. And yeah, I care. It hurts, thinking of you in a situation like that. But it doesn't make me think any less of you, and it sure as hell doesn't make me not want you."

"How can that be?" She's clearly furious with me, and I don't know what to say to fix it. I can't tell her it doesn't bother me at all, because it does, but I also can't tell her that I think she's a terrible person for doing these things.

Most of the time, it's the guys who did this to her who are clearly to blame.

"Think about it," I tell her. "Yeah, maybe you shouldn't have been at those parties. But you were underage, Jenna. You were unconscious. There is no excuse for men doing that to you, no matter what party you went to, or what pills you took."

I'm trying to make it better, but Jenna straightens in her seat. Her eyes narrow. "Do not do that," she says. "Do not make me into a victim just so you can care about me. It was *my* fault. I chose to go to those parties. I *like* them. I always made it clear I was up for anything, so it was my fault. All of it."

My body freezes. I can't breathe. I don't know what to say, because I'm not going to tell her that any of that was her fault. She's been raped, repeatedly, for years, but it feels like an act of violence to force that label on her if she's not ready. I can't do that. It's not my place.

But the fact that she takes full responsibility for all the things that have been done to her kills me. No wonder she thinks I shouldn't want to be with her.

"I'm sorry," I say. "I don't need you to be a victim to care about you. I care about you no matter what you've done."

Jenna's lips press together, and she seems to relax a little. "I might still go to parties," she says. She looks at me for a response, like she wants to know if this is the thing that's going to make me run.

"Would you still hook up with people?" I ask, feeling my heart skip unevenly. She said she's my girlfriend, but maybe that doesn't mean the same thing to her as it does to me.

"No," she says, and I let out a little breath. "I mean, you could come with me, and I could hook up with you."

I smile. "Yeah, okay. But if you're getting black-out drunk, I'm not going to sleep with you."

"Why not?" The edge is back in her voice. "If I told you it was okay beforehand, and then I chose to take pills or whatever,

103

you could do whatever you wanted."

This is never going to happen. Not in a million years. But I don't want to antagonize her again.

"It's not fun for me if you're not awake to be into it," I tell her. "When you're with me, I want you to remember."

The corners of her mouth turn up in a small smile, and I smile back.

I got that much right, at least. "If you still want to go to parties, I want to come with you," I say. "Not because I don't trust you, but just to watch your back."

Jenna nods. "Okay, yeah. But, really, even if you weren't with me, I wouldn't take random pills or drink enough to black out. I wouldn't want anything to happen."

"That makes me feel better," I say. "Otherwise I would worry about you."

She doesn't snap at me about that, and I'm grateful. As much as I *really* don't love the idea of her being with anyone else now, the truth is I'm more worried about what could happen to her when she's unconscious than I am about her actively deciding to cheat on me.

But it still feels damn good to know she doesn't want any of that.

"You'd really do that," she says. "Go with me to a party."

"Yeah. I told you I'd do that the first night we went out."

She looks down at her food. "I shouldn't want to go anymore. But I get so restless sometimes. I might still need to."

"Yeah, okay. I don't get drunk at parties, but I'll come with you anytime."

Jenna looks at me like she's disappointed, but I think my great failure may be that I haven't let her talk me out of being into her, and I'm okay at failing at that.

"Why are you so good to me?" she asks.

She's not asking it in anger. It's a serious question. I look her in the eyes, and I have to tell her. No matter what she says, I just have this feeling she needs to know.

"Because I'm in love with you," I tell her.

Jenna is silent for a long moment, studying me. "I told you not to say that unless you were sure."

"I am sure. More sure than I've ever been of anything."

"Really," she says.

"Yes. I'm sure. I love you."

One corner of her mouth turns up. "I love you, too."

My whole body feels light, as if I might start floating. I wasn't aware of how much I needed to hear that until she said it, and now I can't imagine how I was living without it.

"Yeah?" I say.

"Yeah," she tells me. "A crazy amount."

I reach for her hand across the table again, and she reaches back. "Come home with me," I say. "Come over and stay the night."

Jenna's smile fades, and for a minute, I think she's going to tell me she's not ready. Which should be fine, would be fine, but I don't know how I'm going to take her home and drop her off and let her go. I'll figure it out, I'll—

"What about your parents?" she asks.

I smile. "They go to bed at nine. We won't even run into them."

"But aren't they going to notice if I stay the night?"

"Maybe. But my room is upstairs, and the master suite is downstairs. They won't hear us."

"I can be very loud," Jenna says.

My whole body flushes with heat. I bet she can.

Jenna smiles smugly, and I shake my head at her. She's always known exactly what she does to me.

"And in the morning, if we just act like everything's normal, they aren't going to say anything. In front of you, anyway."

Jenna looks like she can't imagine this is true, but it is. My parents aren't exactly good at confrontation. I get away with a lot on confidence alone.

"Is that what you and Julia did?" she asks.

"No, she never stayed over." I've never pulled this stunt

105

before, but I'm still confident I can do it. "But I did put a hotel room on my dad's credit card once."

"Ha. And your parents didn't say anything?"

"My dad found it on the credit card statement, and he told me I owed him a hundred and twenty dollars. And I said 'Yes, I do.' And then he said he wasn't going to tell my mom, which was code for me to make sure she never knew about it."

Jenna's jaw drops. "And that was it?"

"And that was it."

I fully expect that if I talk Jenna into this, my parents are going to confront me about it eventually. But I'll be able to point out that my dad knew I was having sex, and if my mom didn't, that won't help their position any, because then they'll be mad at each other.

"You could probably stay over at my house, too," Jenna says. "My parents know they can't say anything about what I do, because I'll just ignore them. They wouldn't be thrilled about it, but they'd probably be happy to know where I was."

"You could text them and tell them you're at my house."

Jenna stares at me like this is a ridiculous suggestion. "I *could*."

"And that would probably go a long way toward making them like me—"

"Which they already do. You're right. You're good with parents."

"—and if they like me, it'll make our lives easier."

Jenna sighs. "Fine, I'll come over. And text my parents."

I grin at her. "Don't sound so happy about it."

"You should know," she says, "that half my motivation is because I want to play your grand piano in the morning. And I'm probably going to make us late for school."

"Somehow, I think I'll figure out how to be okay with that."

Jenna smiles at me, and my heart picks up pace.

She's just agreed to stay the night with me. At my house. In my bedroom. And while I'm terrified I'm going to disappoint her, that she's used to an experience I don't know how to provide—

I want so much to make love to her, to show her how much I love and want and respect her. I run my hand over her knee under the table. We both stare into each other's eyes.

I need her, more than I've ever needed anything.

TEN

Jenna

We get back to Felix's house, and he's right; there's no one around or awake to catch us. Though the porch lights are on—for security, I'm guessing—the marble entryway is dark and empty as a tomb, and our footsteps echo just as creepily. We're both on the verge of breaking into giddy laughter that we stifle as we sneak up the stairs, probably with much more caution than we actually need to, given that he's already told me his parents' room is in the other wing.

That's right, wing. This is a house with wings. And marble foyers. And possibly a butler named Alfred lurking around waiting to lead us down the Batcave.

I want to make this joke to Felix—I'm pretty sure he'd laugh—but even with the massive space between us and his parents' room, I'm still terrified of them catching us. I'm scared enough of meeting them in general, but as I'm being snuck into their son's room for sex? Hell no.

Admittedly, I'm nervous right now for other reasons, too, though I'm not entirely sure why. I certainly want him—more than I've ever wanted anyone. And it's not like sex itself is new to me.

But this is sex with Felix. Felix, who's in love with me—a

thought that fills me with so much happiness I feel like I could float away on it. Felix, who I am crazy in love with.

I want to get this right. I mess up so much of my life, but this . . .

I can't bear the thought of losing it.

"Gabby's still out," he says quietly, gesturing towards a dark bedroom with the door cracked open. "Looks like we got lucky."

"If you think that's getting lucky, you haven't seen anything yet," I say, and he laughs, probably more than the joke warrants. I think he's nervous, too.

For the same reason? Or is it something else?

He opens the door to his bedroom and flicks on the light. Earlier today when I was at his house, we pretty much stayed in the sunroom, so this is my first time seeing his room. It's big, easily twice the size of my bedroom, and a hell of a lot cleaner. He's got a queen-sized bed with a deep blue bedspread, neatly made. There are posters on the walls, like in most teen bedrooms, but his are awesome vintage concert posters for bands like Nirvana and the Red Hot Chili Peppers. And, of course, Johnny Cash—which I can only assume must be a reproduction, but maybe not? They are neatly spaced and framed, and it looks like several of them have signatures scrawled across them.

Damn.

His bookshelf is packed with both books and, of course, lots of sheet music. Across the back of his desk chair is the leather jacket I gave him, which I'm more than happy for him to keep. There are some music pages on his desk, with his notes written in pencil, and part of me wants to study them, wants to see every little bow mark and change he's made. Next to those pages is a thick paperback, the same one Rachel was reading the other night, which means it must be for their English class.

It's stupid, but just seeing that book knots my gut up again. I'm not jealous of Rachel, not like that. He clearly wants me. But my dad's words still echo in my head, sharp like heels on marble.

You sure you picked the right daughter?

Felix closes the door behind us and sets his backpack with our baby down on his desk, right on top of the book like he barely notices it's there.

There's a pause where we eye each other, and we're smiling. I'm dying to touch him, but my nerves feel all exposed. He tugs his lower lip between his teeth, and I can't help but ask, "You really want this, right? Tonight? If you wanted to wait for me to get an STD test, I'd understand."

I feel my cheeks flush, even though I *would* totally understand. He had a point about that being a good idea. I may have been a bit hyperbolic when I practically yelled at him about how many guys I'd been with just this past weekend (the real answer? two), but it's not like I haven't had weeks like that before. Plenty of times. All of the guys I've been with since I got tested last month used condoms, and I didn't have any blackouts during that time that would make me question any unaccounted-for sex,.so I think I'm clean.

It's embarrassing, though, how often I'm not sure.

He lets out a breath and steps forward, pulling me into his arms. "God, yes, I want this tonight. So much." There's this depth of feeling in his voice, this longing, and I know he means it. My nerves settle down a bit, replaced by a heady warmth. "We'll use protection; it'll be fine. And it's not just you that needs the test, right?"

I give him a knowing look, but don't argue. The truth is, I appreciate the gesture, even though I am as worried about picking up an STD from him as I am of dying by meteor strike. "Sure," I say.

"What about you? You really want this too, yeah?"

I smile, and tip up to kiss him, deeply. I pour all my need for him, physical and otherwise, in that kiss, into the way my hands roam up his shirt and across the back of his neck up into his hair. He responds with the same need, the same desperate desire, our tongues brushing, our bodies pressed together, that

110

heat between us—heat that flares so naturally and so brightly—burning and burning.

As one, we start towards the bed, with me backing up, our lips not straying from each other, our hands tangled in hair and stroking the skin under our shirts. The backs of my knees have just grazed the comforter when he pulls off my black tank top, dropping it on the floor, and his fingers run along the lacy edge of my dark purple bra, sending shivers through me.

I tug his shirt off as well, pulling him down with me as I sit, and then lie back on the bed, and oh, how incredible it feels with the weight of him on me, the heat of his skin against mine. The feel of him hard between my legs, even through his jeans and my skirt. His mouth begins working its way down my neck, slowly, and then his lips caress the tops of my breasts, and I'm already making little gasping sounds, my whole body alight with every touch, every breath.

My fingers move down from the muscles of his back, and just barely dip below his pants, eliciting a similar sound from him, and I'm about to explore further when a baby starts wailing from a backpack across the room.

Felix groans, squeezing his eyes shut. "Seriously?"

I couldn't agree more, though I can't help but laugh at the timing.

He starts kissing at the crook of my neck, which makes my whole body hum. "I vote for ignoring her," he murmurs against my skin. "Let her cry herself back to sleep or whatever."

I prop myself up with my elbows. "No way, man. Ninety percent or I don't get paid, remember?"

He groans again, but good-naturedly, and rolls off me, and goes to fetch the kid, though his gait is a bit . . . stiff. I can't help but grin, even as my body strongly protests the absence of his.

He picks up the baby and pats it, a little more aggressively than necessary. "You know, kid, you're never going to get an android brother or sister if you keep interrupting your mom and me."

I laugh, but my whole body flushes. I know it's just a joke, but him talking like that, like we're this family . . . It's that same feeling of watching him play with Ty, this perfect melting happiness and this pulsing anxiety all at the same time. Longing that goes way beyond the physical, and fear that cuts bone-deep.

I think of him asking if I want to really be Ty's mom. Offering to help me with that, as if maybe he thinks he might want to be part of that future someday.

I don't know if I can believe I'm capable of being Ty's mom in reality. I don't know if that's something that can actually happen, no matter what I do or how hard I try—like I said at dinner, I'm not sure it works like that, especially with someone like me, who is about as far from mom material as you can get.

But I know I want to get *this* right, with Felix, whatever future that eventually leads to.

I try to breathe normally, which isn't easy given how my body is still all reactive from his touch just moments before. I take the opportunity to unlace my boots and kick them off, flexing my toes against the deep carpeting.

Felix finally gets the baby to be quiet again, setting her down on top of his backpack, and smiles at me. There's this moment where he just takes me in, sitting on the edge of his bed, in my bra and skirt, and the stark wanting in that gaze makes me ache and ache.

I long to keep that wanting I see in him. For him to feel it even after we've had sex, for him to still want me like this, to still *love* me, even when this isn't new anymore.

I need to get this right.

Felix

When I put the baby down and look back at Jenna again, this surreal moment passes over me—that's Jenna Rollins on my bed, and she's half-dressed, and in love with me, and I'm in love with her.

She wants me.

Jenna Rollins wants me.

I'm not sure I'll ever get used to that.

Jenna climbs to her knees as I come back to the bed, and runs her palms up my chest, sending shivers through my body. She gives me this look, and it's sexy, but there's something off about it. Her mouth works the skin under my ear, and my body responds, and I wrap my hands around her waist again, pulling her to me.

Her voice is low in my ear. "How do you want it?"

I tense. She sounds like a girl in a porno, more so as she continues. "I can do anything you want, Felix. I can go down on you, or you can take me from behind. If you like anal, I'm good with—"

I pull away from her, my heart pounding. I want her, yeah, but not like some kind of playboy fantasy. Not that her words don't turn me on at all, but in a twisted way that just feels wrong.

I don't want it to be like this. Not ever. "What are you doing?" I ask.

Jenna leans back on her heels, suddenly nervous. She looks at me like she's scared, and it breaks my heart. "I just—what do you want me to be for you?"

God, this is what she's used to. Men who want to use her like a toy, who want her to meet their specific demands, who want her to play out their fantasies like some kind of true-to-life doll. Just the thought of it makes me want to cry. I take her face in my hands. "Jenna, I want you to be you. That's all I want. Just to be with *you*."

She stares at me, like this is a revelation, and my chest aches for her.

"Okay," she says, but she pulls away. "Give me a couple minutes, okay?"

"Yeah, sure," I tell her, but I have no idea what she means. She kisses me softly and then climbs off the bed and heads into the bathroom and closes the door between us.

I have no idea what's happening. My body is starting to ache all over from longing, and there's this knot in my chest, because I'm messing this up. God, the last thing I want is to be messing this up.

I hear the water running, and I collapse on the bed, sitting against the headboard and trying to breathe. I take off my shoes and then close my eyes.

It's going to be okay.

It has to be okay.

But what if she comes out of there and she doesn't want me anymore? What if I've just messed everything up? Have I asked too much of her? I should have thought that she probably wants different things out of this than I do. She probably wants someone assertive, someone who knows what he wants, who has any clue how to do some of the things she describes. I mean, I get the concept, but still. I probably sounded so naive.

I'm an idiot.

Jenna

I stand in the bathroom, looking at myself in the mirror, my heart pounding against my rib cage.

He wants me. As I am. Jenna Rollins. Felix Mays wants *me*.

And I want to give that to him.

I start pulling the hair pins out of my crazy Mickey Mouse buns, letting my black hair fall down past my shoulders. There's not much I can do about the artificial color, but while I know the buns are a passing stylistic choice (one I like, but mainly started doing just to see what weird-ass hairstyle I could get away with and still look hot), I think I'm always going to want to dye my hair dark.

Then I get a washcloth and start scrubbing off my makeup. I like makeup, and I know I tend to wear more of it than I need—black eyeliner, mascara, usually some sort of bold eyeshadow, lipstick and gloss, the whole thing. I like putting it on before parties, or before school, piece by piece like armor.

But I want to take it off, for him.

I want him to see the eyelashes that aren't naturally a mile long, and the lips that are a hair thin, and the faint sprinkle of freckles across the bridge of my nose. Not for always—it's not like I'm giving up makeup and becoming some hippie earth-goddess, god no.

But for tonight, I want to make sure he sees *me*.

As I wash my face—a couple times, because I don't necessarily want him to see mascara-smudged raccoon eyes—I can't help think of the times I do this when I'm home after a party. The times I look at myself in the mirror, the makeup stripped away, the clothes bunched on the tiles, party Jenna some girl who lived a night I can barely remember. And I wonder what

I must look like to all of them, this trashy girl getting wasted and passing out, waking up covered in articles of some dude's clothes. Or sometimes nothing at all.

A thing to be used. To be left behind and forgotten, like that jacket.

I think of how I erupted at Felix back at dinner and cringe. I need him to see that I've made these choices, that I've been the person who does this and keeps going back. Because I'm so afraid that if he sees me as some victim, sees me as better than I am, then he'll leave when he learns the truth is what I've been telling him all along.

But maybe.

Maybe he can love me—this girl, as she is.

And maybe that can help me be more.

I set the wet washcloth down and dry my face on a towel. Then I strip off my skirt, so I'm in my bra and underwear—not a matching set sadly, and my underwear isn't as sexy as the bra, since I wasn't expecting we'd have sex today. I consider going out naked, but I want to experience *him* taking off the rest.

I let out a shaky breath.

Me, I think. This is me.

And, still unaccountably afraid of what he'll think, I open the bathroom door and step out.

Felix

startle as the door to the bathroom opens, and Jenna stands in the doorway with her hair down. Her skirt is gone, and her underwear cuts up high on her hips, framing her thighs. Her hair is down, hanging in soft waves, and her face is clean, all her makeup washed away.

She's so incredibly beautiful. I climb to my feet as she approaches, reaching out and running a hand down her face.

Jenna looks gorgeous in makeup, and I kind of like the ridiculous buns with her hair sticking out every which way. But she looks more real now, more vulnerable, and I can't help but whisper her name. I brush my thumb across her lips, and she closes her eyes.

I can't take it anymore. I want to stare at her for hours, like she's a work of art, a painting, but I need to be with her, up close, with nothing between us. I run my hands through her hair and pull her to me, kissing her softly, and then with growing need. Her hands dig into my back, and I've had enough of these clothes between us. I unhook her bra, and pull it down, and then her chest presses against mine, soft and warm, and she's moaning against my lips and I can't breathe, god, I can't breathe. We roll onto the bed and she tumbles over me until she's lying on her side with one leg hooked around my waist. I reach down and run a hand up the back of her thigh and up under the elastic of her panties. We kiss like we'll never break apart, and then she's working down my chest again, like she did in the car, only this time I'm feeling so much more, so much deeper, even though I never would have thought it was possible then.

Jenna

We're kissing, and we're exploring, and there's this strange and amazing sense of desperate rush and need combined with the feeling that we have all the time in the world, that this perfect little bubble of sensation and heat can last forever, just the two of us.

I begin kissing down his chest again like I did in the car, but this time when I reach his pants, I start to unbutton them, and he helps me, shrugging out of his jeans until he's just in his boxer briefs, and I reach inside those, feeling the hard length of him, aching with each little gasp and moan my touch brings out. And then he's doing the same with me, those sexy cello-string-calloused fingers dipping down beneath my underwear, teasing, lighting gently in places that make me see little stars behind my eyelids. I start tugging off my underwear, and he doesn't hesitate to help, using the motion to run his fingers down along my leg again and back, up and up.

I want him inside me with a desperate need I've never felt before with anyone else, not even close.

Because I'm starting to understand now, the difference between sex and making love, and I know I've only ever done the one and always, always longed for the other, even if I would never have admitted it myself.

Even if I never felt worthy of it.

I sit back, and he sits up with me, and I guide him gently, like a dancer leading her partner, so that he's sitting up with his back against the headboard again. I tug down his underwear, and notice the condom on the nightstand that I'm guessing he got out while I was in the bathroom. I straddle his lap, allowing myself the briefest sensation of him against me if not yet in me, which causes his eyelids to flutter, and mine as well. Then I tear open the condom, and begin rolling it on him, slowly, in a way that makes him groan.

He opens his eyes again when it's on, and he's got this expression of wonder, like he could stare at me forever.

Felix

The tension is so thick I feel like I might snap, but at the same time I want to stretch it on and on and on. I stare into her eyes, gray like the sea on a cloudy day, and the heat and pleasure coursing through me mixes with this brightness, this light, and it's the most beautiful thing I've ever felt. I reach up and stroke her breast, and her lips part, and I feel like we're connected, she and I, even though I'm not yet inside her. "You're so, so beautiful," I tell her. "Everything about you is beautiful." And I don't know that I'm supposed to be having this strangely aesthetic experience while my girlfriend is straddling me, but it feels so good, I don't even care.

Tears form in her eyes. "I love you," she whispers.

"I love you, Jenna," I respond, and my eyes are burning. We are about to be two idiots who cry before having sex, but Jenna saves us by easing me inside her. The world collapses around us, all matter in the universe bearing down until we're tight, so tight together. We move gently at first, but the sensation is overpowering, and I'm crying out, and so is she as she arches against me.

Jenna

My whole body burns brighter and brighter as I slowly ease myself onto him. That in itself makes me cry out softly, and we begin to move together, gently at first, taking our time. And I understand even more how this is different from all the rest.

With others, sex was just like the alcohol or pills, nothing more or less—something to numb me from the shame of the night before, this endless cycle of fake pleasure and dull, relentless pain.

With him, it's not about taking away feelings. It's about experiencing them in this real and intense way—feeling the way he sees me, the way he loves me, the way I see and love him. The sensation of everything we are to each other, everything we might yet be.

And it's incredible.

Felix

We're staring into each other's eyes, and I feel as if I'm being swallowed up in her, like we're one person, body and soul. I hold her against me, and her hands dig through my hair, and we move faster and faster, tension pulling like a well-tuned string, vibrating up and down with the purest notes in the world. Our bodies play each other like instruments, rising toward a grand crescendo. Jenna peaks seconds before I do, crying out my name as her whole body shudders, and her pleasure travels through me, vibrating faster until it snaps and I'm the one crying out, my whole being fractured apart and filled with a blinding light, and then shuddering beneath her.

We hold each other, breathing hard, our bodies slick with sweat. I press my face in to her neck, astounded at how beautiful that was, how powerful. "God, I love you so much," I say, and I press my lips to her skin.

"Right back at you," she says, and though her voice trembles, she's soft and relaxed in my arms. "So much."

I shake my head, still struck with wonder. "That was . . . that was amazing."

JeNNA

"All the amazing," I agree, though I don't know that words exist to describe the intensity of being with him like that. I try a few more words, though, anyway. "And hot as *hell*."

He laughs. "Yeah. I definitely agree with *that*. Oh my god." He laughs again, like he can't believe this happened, and I laugh with him. Then I roll off him so I can curl up against his side, tucked under his arm. My heart is still hammering against my ribs, and I wonder if he can feel it. I can feel his heart pounding under my hand, and it makes me stupidly happy.

We lie there for several long, perfect minutes, just holding each other, stroking each other lightly—him along my waist, and me, along his arm and down his chest—breathing each other in.

And though it's probably weird to bring this up now, of all times, I find myself saying it anyway.

"I think I'd really like it if we took Ty to the park," I say. "Just you and me and him, you know?" A flush burns my cheeks the minute the words come out. *Exactly* what a guy wants to hear right after sex, I'm sure. "I mean, not that there's any pressure, and it doesn't have to be soon. And if you didn't want to, that's okay. I don't mean—"

"Jenna, hey," he says, squeezing my arm. "I offered, remember?" He smiles at me. "I think that sounds awesome. He's a great kid. And I kind of want to spend every minute I can with you."

I smile back, relieved. "Yeah, okay. I kind of want to spend every minute with you, too."

And as we lie there, talking some more, and then working each other up for another round, I can't help but wish, crazy though it might be, that we weren't talking in minutes, but in years.

Maybe even in lifetimes.

ELEVEN

Felix

I'm lying in bed with Jenna, holding her, thinking that I'm not sure how this perfect thing descended on me in so short a time, and I have no idea how I can ever be worthy of it, when I hear my sister Gabby march up the stairs outside my room.

Jenna freezes, and I pull her closer. Gabby will probably just go to bed. It's late, and even though my bedside lamp is still on, most nights she doesn't—

There's a loud rap on my bedroom door. "Felix!" Gabby shouts. "Oh my god you will not believe the day I've had." She pauses, and Jenna and I look at each other. Jenna looks like she wants to slide under the covers and disappear, but I shake my head at her.

"Hang on!" I yell back. My parents are at the far other end of the house, on a different floor, in a different wing. They aren't going to hear us, and even if they could, they wouldn't do anything about it.

"Hurry up!" Gabby says. "You've been gone and I didn't even get to tell you about how I set fire to a microwave before I got fired for it. And then I went on this date tonight that was supposed to make me feel better. Spoiler, Felix. It did not."

"Should I hide in the bathroom?" Jenna asks quietly, grabbing frantically for her scattered clothes.

"No," I whisper back. Gabby's going to be surprised about my relationship with Jenna, and possibly worried. But I know she'll come around eventually. Gabby's got the best heart in the world, and she'll see how good Jenna is for me, even if it takes her a while. "But if you want to borrow a shirt or something, you're welcome to." I pull open a dresser drawer for her so she doesn't have to worry about finding her clothes, and put my own shirt and pants back on.

I open the door a crack and stand in front of it. Gabby raises her eyebrows at me, and stares at my head. I'm guessing I have a raging case of sex hair. "I was also on a date," I tell her with a pointed look. "It went really well."

Gabby's eyes bug out and she takes a step back. Then, in the loudest stage whisper ever, she says, "Do you have a girl in there?"

I laugh and look over my shoulder. Jenna is sitting awkwardly at the end of my bed wearing my Meat Puppets t-shirt and a pair of my flannel boxers, and looking hotter than hell in them. I'm guessing this reaction registers on my face, because Jenna smiles nervously at me. I sigh and swing the door open. "Jenna, meet my sister Gabby. Gabby, have you met Jenna? She's my girlfriend that I'm completely and totally in love with."

From the look of pure shock on her face, I'm guessing Gabby at least knows *of* Jenna. Gabby was three years ahead of me in school, so she was a junior when Jenna was a freshman.

Jenna waves awkwardly. "Hey."

"I didn't know you had a girlfriend," Gabby says.

"Yeah, that's new," I say. "Today, actually."

Gabby looks from Jenna to me with an expression of horror on her face.

Okay. So maybe she's going to be more than a little bit worried. "Felix," she says, "can I talk to you in my room?"

I turn back to Jenna. She's folding in on herself, and I don't want to leave her alone to worry that my sister is going to talk me out of being with her. She couldn't, even if she tried.

"Why don't we talk in here?" I say. "I'm going to tell Jenna about it anyway." I walk to the bed and wrap Jenna in my arms, and Gabby stares at us like she's got no idea what to do with this. But she's my sister, so she pulls out my desk chair, and admirably tries to ignore Jenna's bra on the floor and—oh shit—the used condoms on the nightstand, which I should have done something about before this moment, and gives us a forced smile.

"So," Gabby says, "how long have you guys been seeing each other?"

Gabby's surprise is fair. I usually tell her about the girls I'm into, and always talk to her about whoever I'm dating. It's not that I've been hiding Jenna from her. This week has just been . . . busy. "We were paired together on a health project," I say, just as the baby on the desk starts wailing again. Gabby's eyes go wide and she pushes the chair away from the sound, like the baby is going to bite her. I get up and go over to retrieve it.

"Oh, yeah," Gabby says. "I remember that assignment. It was a nightmare."

"Right?" Jenna says. "That thing never stops."

"You guys are in the same health class?" Gabby asks.

"Yeah," I tell her, moving on before Jenna feels like she has to explain why. "And we got paired to work together, and started talking for the first time. Sorry I didn't tell you, Gabs. This week has been crazy."

"That's the truth," Jenna says.

I bring the baby over to the bed and pat her again, until she calms down.

"I don't remember mine having such cute pajamas," Gabby says, and I'm grateful, because I don't want Ty to be the elephant in the room.

"They belonged to Jenna's son. He's adorable, but a little big for them now."

Gabby stares at me, looking like she's going to explode from unanswered questions. I'm realizing maybe I should have gone with her into her room, because while Gabby is usually pretty averse to confrontation, I'm not sure how many concerns even she can hold in under these circumstances.

"Excuse me," Jenna says, and she gets up and goes into the bathroom.

I'm assuming this is calculated to give me time to get rid of my sister, or at least convince her to breathe so her face stops turning as red as a tomato. "Hey," I say. "Don't freak out. It's okay."

"It's *okay*?" Gabby asks. "How can it be okay? You're dating *Jenna Rollins*? You're *in love* with her?"

"I am, Gabs. I know what people say about Jenna. Hell, I thought the same things everyone else does. And yeah, she's got a past, and a kid, and she's done a lot of partying. But she's *awesome*, and she loves me, and we're really, incredibly happy."

Gabby looks at the closed bathroom door, like she can't imagine how this could be, but she nods. "But she's got a *kid*. Doesn't that scare you?"

I think about that. There are a lot of things about being with Jenna that scare me. "A little. Honestly, the whole relationship scares me, because it's more real than anything I've ever felt. But Jenna is awesome, and you're going to love her, seriously. But could you do me a favor and stop scaring the hell out of her?"

Gabby blinks at me. "I'm scaring Jenna Rollins. Me."

"Yeah," I say. "Because she's already worried about what Mom and Dad are going to think of her—"

"Ha," Gabby says. "With good reason. They are going to kill you."

"I know. So would you please keep your title as best sister ever and be nice to my girlfriend? Please?"

Gabby presses her lips together. "She's really your girlfriend? I never got the impression she . . . dated people. Especially not seriously."

"She didn't," I say. "Not before me. And we're both a little stunned at how fast this happened, so you're not alone in that."

Gabby's eyes flick to the condoms again, and she grimaces.

"Oh, my god, yes, I'm having sex with her. Can we please not freak out about that? You know I'm not a virgin, so just don't get on my case about it, okay?"

I can tell what Gabby's thinking. I could have this argument with myself. Yeah, it was one thing when I was sleeping with Julia after months of dating her, but it's something else for me to start sleeping with Jenna after a couple of days. Besides which, Gabby herself is a virgin, so sex seems like a bigger deal to her than it's ever been to me.

Before Jenna, that is.

"Is she staying over?" Gabby asks.

"Yeah," I say.

"And Mom and Dad don't know."

I give her a look. "I announced it to them over dinner. *Of course* they don't know."

"What if they catch you?"

"They aren't going to catch us," I say, "because we aren't going to hide from them. They'll figure it out in the morning, and then the freak out will begin. But it's coming anyway, and I don't know what I can do about it."

The bathroom door opens, and Jenna comes out and sits on my bed right between the nightstand and Gabby, probably to hide the condoms. Gabby smiles at her, and this time it's hesitant but genuine, which is a big improvement. "Sorry for intruding on you guys. I usually have a better idea what's going on in Felix's life."

"Yeah," Jenna says. "And sorry about your . . . microwave fire."

"They really let you go over that?" I ask. "That seems unfair. I'm guessing it was their crappy microwave at fault."

Gabby waves a hand like it's nothing, but I know it isn't. She had a crush on her boss, who I'm guessing is the one who fired her.

Wait.

"Were you on a date with that Will guy?" I ask.

"No," Gabby says. "He didn't fire me and ask me out in the same breath, although that would still have been better than the guy I *did* have a date lined up with." She shrugs. "Whatever. I'm going to bed. Maybe I'll wake up tomorrow and meet a guy who doesn't think taking me to a tailgate party counts as a financial commitment that requires sexual repayment."

I cringe. "Ouch. Sorry, Gabs."

She shrugs again. "Good luck with Mom and Dad," she says, and she leaves, closing the door to my room behind her.

Jenna collapses on the bed. "She hates me. And your parents are going to hate me even more."

I curl up next to her, sliding my hands under the shirt she's wearing, along the smooth skin of her back. "Hey," I say. "Gabby was just surprised. I would have told her about you already, but I haven't exactly been home much the last couple of days. Wonder why."

Jenna looks doubtful. "I remember Gabby. She always seemed cool. I just wish she didn't obviously remember *me*."

"Gabby doesn't know you. But she will, and she'll like you. Trust me, I know my sister."

"And the rest of your family?"

I take a deep breath. "The rest of my family doesn't give a shit about me. All they care about are my grades and my music, and making sure I become some famous cellist that my mother can brag about to her brunch friends. I haven't *seen* my parents in three days, and they haven't noticed. That'll tell you how involved they are in my life."

Jenna wraps herself around me, holding me, and I close my eyes. I hadn't meant to say all of that to her. I try not to think about it most of the time, because there's nothing to be done about it. Gabby and I care about each other. All anyone else in my family cares about is appearances.

"I'm sorry," Jenna says. "That sucks."

I hold her back, breathing in the scent of her hair, running my hands up and down her back. "Also," I say, "you look incredibly sexy in my clothes."

"Mmm," Jenna says, rolling over on top of me. "Is that so?"

"It is. And Gabby will come around. But she's also not likely to interrupt us again tonight."

Jenna smiles as I lift my shirt off over her head. "Well, then," she says. "It would be a shame to let that opportunity go to waste."

I wake up in the morning with Jenna wrapped tight in my arms, our legs tangled together. My memories of last night are at once vivid and fuzzy—the thrill of making love to her woven in with the content happiness of drifting off to sleep together.

I kiss her temple, and she rolls over to face me. "Morning, gorgeous," I say.

"Morning," she answers. "What time is it?"

"Early. But you wanted to play the piano, and I'm not going to let you make me *too* late for school."

Jenna wraps her arms around my neck and kisses me. "We'll see about that."

Half an hour later we're standing at the counter in the kitchen, unable to keep our hands off each other even to eat cornflakes. Jenna's wearing the same clothes she had on yesterday, and I'm wearing new ones, kissing her neck between bites of cereal and pulling her body against mine, feeling every inch of her through her clothes. Jenna spills a spoonful of milk down my arm, but it's worth it. Even just eating breakfast with her, I'm floating, and I'm not looking forward to taking her to school and going to class without her. Even the robotic baby on the counter seems content.

A voice clears in the kitchen doorway, and I look up to see my dad standing there, already in his suit and briefcase for work. He's watching Jenna and me with sharp eyes, and I grin at him.

"Hey, Dad. Have you met my girlfriend? This is Jenna."

There's no particular recognition in his eyes. I gather he doesn't have a clue who Jenna is, and that's good, though my mom is likely to ask around and figure it out sooner or later. "Hello, Jenna," he says. "Good morning, Felix."

There's an edge to his voice, but as I expected, he turns and walks away. He'll probably pick up breakfast on his way to work, as he often does, and I'm willing to bet we'll be talking about this later.

"Wow," Jenna says. "He really doesn't care that I'm here."

"Told you," I say. I meant what I said last night, about my parents not really caring about me. "My parents will talk to each other about it, and then I'll get an earful, but it's not going to stop us from doing this again."

I don't mention that the earful is much more likely to be about the particular girl I'm sleeping with than the fact that I'm seventeen and having sex. But if I'm going to have to put up with my parents being jerks about me being with Jenna, I'm sure as hell going to take full advantage of the perks.

TWELVE

Jenna

We get to school after a quick stop at my house so I can change. Not that I mind everyone seeing me in yesterday's clothes and knowing what's up—god knows Felix's family certainly does now—but I am fond of personal hygiene and clean underwear. Besides, it's not like everyone at school doesn't figure what's up pretty quick, when Felix and I hold hands in the hallway, or when he catches me on his way to orchestra for a quick kiss that even more quickly becomes a make out against a row of lockers outside the music room.

I playfully push him away as the warning bell rings, grinning, and he shakes his head, grinning back, but then ducks into the classroom. I've already cost him enough cello practice, and it's not like we don't have plenty of incredible make-outs and even more incredible sex ahead of us. All the time in the world, maybe.

Felix is my boyfriend.

Felix loves me.

I can't shake the dopey smile on my face, especially when I see another prom poster, and imagine us there, just next week—dancing and laughing and just being us, every incredible thing that we are together and to each other.

I try not to think about the fact that I'll be graduating only weeks later, and have no idea what in hell I'm doing with my life. But whatever it is, it'll be here.

We'll have all the time in the world.

I hear some snickering and see Angela and Julia and a couple other girls on their way into the music room, giving me that mean-girls look cliques tend to sync as naturally as their periods.

"Such a white-trash whore," Angela says to Julia in a voice that carries way too well to actually be the murmur she pretends. She twists the ends of her curly red hair as she glares at me.

Julia's lips curl into a smirk. Her big blue eyes only cut to me for the barest second, like I'm not even worth the energy of a glare. "Hope he triple-bags it."

I usually say something smart-ass back to comments like Julia's—"Well, we used three last night, but definitely not all at once," seems appropriate here—but something stops me, and I just walk by like I didn't even notice them.

It takes me a minute before I realize that I actually feel bad for Julia. Sure, she's annoying as hell and kind of a bitch—she's called me a slut or a skank on more than one occasion, even before I'd ever spoken to Felix, though I suppose she's far from alone in that. But the truth is, I can't imagine how it must feel to have been with Felix, to think he really loved me and then find out I was wrong.

Or really, I guess, I *can* imagine it. And I'm not sure anything could rip my heart out more than that.

I don't blame Felix for it, because I know he thought he loved her, and hormones, as I know well, can be pretty damn convincing. He'd never have purposefully hurt someone like that. But really, no one deserves that kind of pain. Not even bitchy flutists.

I don't tell Felix about my run-in with his former fan club; honestly, it's not like it's any worse for me than usual, if a little more directly aimed at my dating one of their own. I wonder if he's gotten any shit yet. I'm not sure if he'd voluntarily tell me, any more than I did.

What I do know, especially after last night, is that even if he did and even if it sucked worse than he anticipated, he'd still want to be with me.

Felix loves me, and it feels like nothing short of a miracle.

It's that feeling that gets me through our trip to Planned Parenthood for testing without guilt overcoming me. Well, that and his continued insistence that he really just wants to make sure I'm okay for my own health. He treats the whole experience like it's nothing big, just a precaution, nothing to feel shame over. Like it's something he should have done long before now anyway. And though we both know that's total crap, it's nice that he's so determined to make this okay for me. That he's in this with me, all the way.

This is even more apparent when we leave Planned Parenthood and he grins over at me. "So it's a pretty nice day out," he says. "The kind of afternoon that's perfect for taking a kid to the park."

My chest squeezes in a bit. "Today?" What I really mean is *already?*

He gives a half-shrug. "Sure. If you'd be up for it."

It was one thing to feel like I was capable of taking baby steps towards the mom thing last night, emboldened by love and the best sex of my life. Probably I could have claimed with equal belief that I was ready to climb Mount Kilimanjaro in flip-flops.

But now, with the possibility of it being, well, *now . . .*

He smiles gently and takes my hand. "We don't have to. Whenever you're ready is good with me."

"What about your practice?"

"I figure I can get in a couple hours later tonight. Before bed." He says that last bit with enough meaning that I know perfectly well he's hoping I'll be joining him again, and god knows I don't need to be implied at twice.

I smile back. "I wouldn't mind some pre-bedtime serenading. Except it'll probably put me in the mood for things other than sleep."

"That's the plan." He runs his thumb over my knuckles.

And something about the ease of just being with him, the comfort of his hand on mine . . . I feel that courage coming back.

After all, it's just an afternoon with two of us and a toddler. Who is adorable and funny and a really good kid. How hard can that be?

I try not to remember how we forgot our robot baby on a ride at Disneyland.

"Okay, yeah," I say. "Let's take him today."

We drive back to my house. Rachel, thankfully, isn't there to give me any more crap about letting Ty get too attached to Felix. But my mom is, and her reaction to me asking if we could take Ty to the park isn't as uncertain and wary as I was expecting. Downright shocked, yes. And then . . . strangely gleeful.

"Oh, that sounds wonderful! Ty loves the park! Don't you, Ty?"

Ty doesn't answer. He's sitting in front of the TV, mesmerized by this weird-ass kids show with these giant friendly monsters singing on some retro-70's soundstage about how all food wants to have a party in your tummy. Once I thought I saw Jack Black on an episode, joining in.

I'm pretty sure the creators of this are constantly high.

Mom sighs, but she's still got this way-too-wide smile plastered on her face. "He definitely needs some outside time," she says. "I'll pack up some things for him, and give you the directions to his favorite park."

I had no idea he had a favorite park. Aren't they all kind of the same? Swings, slides, climbing structures covered in boogers.

"Great," I say, though it comes out a little weak. Felix notices and gives me an encouraging smile.

Mom grabs the big bag she always takes with her when she and Ty go out. I know it's always jam-packed full of stuff, but I haven't paid much attention to what exactly. But now—

"There are diapers in here, and wipes, of course," she says, opening the bag and indicating each item jutting crazily out of an insane number of inside pockets. "And there's an extra outfit, in case of accidents. And there's Band-Aids and Neosporin, you know, just in case. And hand sanitizer—you'll want to make sure he uses that before he has a snack—oh, I need to re-fill the snack baggie!" She sets the bag down and hurries into the kitchen.

Oh my god. Are we taking Ty to the park, or on a cross-country road trip? How much of this will we actually need?

I'm at least marginally grateful that Felix's eyes look about as wide as mine.

Grateful, that is, until the thought crosses my mind that maybe this will freak him out, that maybe he's regretting offering to help me with this. I wouldn't blame him—Ty isn't some robot baby we can leave in Felix's backpack while we go make out. And I have no idea if I can manage even a small trip to the park without messing the kid up somehow.

My mom bustles back in the living room, with several small baggies of snacks—Cheerios, pretzels, raisins—and one of Ty's sippy cups. "You'll need to put his car seat in Felix's car," she says, gesturing to the car seat that sits by the front door. We only have one car, and Dad drives it to work, so mom keeps the car seat here in case she gets a ride with someone to the store or something and needs it.

"Yeah, sure," Felix says, picking up the car seat. He looks at it and the mass of buckles and straps hanging down from it like it's a bomb about to detonate if he doesn't clip the right wire.

Mom laughs. "I'll show you how to buckle it in. Come on."

There's a tutorial of strapping the car seat into the back seat of Felix's Toyota that involves way too many clips. Not to mention so much tugging to make sure the thing is tightly secured that there's a decent chance it's now permanently attached to Felix's leather seat. Both Felix and I look a little dazed when it's over and Mom hands me the bulging bag—which feels like it weighs more than Ty somehow—and straps Ty into the car seat.

"Have fun!" she says brightly.

"Park!" Ty cheers.

"Park," Felix agrees, and gives me a smile, which I return, nervously, my knuckles white as they clutch the diaper bag.

We drive to the park, and Ty sings the song about the party in his tummy from that wacked-out show.

"So your mom seemed pretty happy about us taking him out," Felix says, his eyes cutting over to me.

"She's probably happy to get some free time," I say with a little laugh. But my stomach is churning like it's having its own party, and not a particularly fun one. The truth is, I could tell my mom was really excited about me making this small gesture of responsibility with Ty. This baby step towards being his mom in more than name.

That she's wanted this from me is something I always suspected, but to see that bright hope in her eyes—

Maybe some people would be encouraged by that hope, but it just makes me feel panicky and horribly inadequate.

Ty's favorite park, apparently, is about a ten-minute drive from my house, in a neighborhood that's a small step up from ours and still about a dozen steps down from Brentwood. The park itself has a baseball diamond being used for little league practice and a basketball court being used as an ad-hoc skate park, but Ty ignores them both and darts toward the playground—particularly a bright blue submarine about ten feet long and four feet tall.

There are already several kids playing in the thing, and all of them are bigger than him. Is he going to get trampled in there?

"Ty, don't you want to do the swings?" I try, shifting the big diaper bag higher on my shoulder. "Or how about you ride this thing?" I wiggle the plastic saddle-like seat attached to one of those big metal coils so it wobbles back and forth.

Ty runs back to me and grabs my hand, tugging me towards the submarine as he points. "Submaneen! Mom, it's a sub-maneen!"

"The kid knows what he wants," Felix says with a laugh. He's got his backpack with our robot baby in it, so technically we're taking two kids to the park today.

"I guess so," I say, but I'm wondering how long it's been since Ty's tugged my hand like this. How long since I've felt his little chubby fingers wrapped around mine? A few weeks, at least. Have I really spent that little time with him? Guilt wraps around my heart.

Baby steps.

I give his hand a little squeeze as I let him pull me forward.

He climbs the two stairs into the submarine, and I stand right behind him in case he falls or gets pushed back, trying not to give death glares to the other kids who get too close. But Ty weaves through them and finds an unmanned periscope, which he turns and turns. Felix gets on the other side of the submarine, and peers through a porthole by Ty, rapping on the "glass" with his knuckles until Ty turns and sees him. Felix makes a face, and Ty giggles, and I find myself laughing along with him—it's such a contagious, purely happy sound.

Felix and Ty play this game a while longer, while I anxiously watch through the submarine "door"—which is really a huge opening nearly half the length of the submarine itself, and is probably how this thing keeps from becoming a deathtrap of heat and poopy diaper stench—and cringe every time a kid pushes past him. Ty barely notices, though, too busy making faces back at Felix and giggling louder and louder.

After he's done with the submarine, Ty's ready for the swings, and then the slide. He takes on both with a total lack of fear, just this boundless glee. He wants Felix—or "Fee-yix," as he calls him—to push him on the swing, but doesn't want either of us helping him on the slide, and yells out for us both to "Look at me! Look at me!" every time he's about to go down.

We're both playing with him, and it's actually kind of fun, but no matter what I do, I can't shake this awkwardness. Like everything I'm doing, every time I'm saying "Good job, Ty!" or

"Yeah, that *is* a ladybug" or whatever, I'm really just some actress reading from a script for a part there's no way in hell I'm getting.

Felix, on the other hand, doesn't seem to have this problem. "It's Super Ty!" he yells at one point, picking Ty up and swooping him around, which causes another eruption of those giggles, and then another twenty minutes of Ty begging "Fee-yix, scoop me! Scoop me, Fee-yix!" no matter how many times Felix swoops him. It's freaking adorable, and yet something in me aches painfully at the sight.

"What have I done?" Felix asks me with a chuckle, shaking his undoubtedly sore arms out.

"Become Ty's new best friend." I smile, but even I can feel how it's forced. Felix's own smile slips.

"Scoop me, Fee-yix!" Ty tries again, reaching for Felix, but Felix crouches down next to him.

"My arms are tired, kid. How about you ask your mom to do Super Ty?"

"No! You do it!" Ty demands, his little brow furrowing.

"It's okay," I say, ignoring the little stab in my chest. "Ty, look! The submarine's free. Do you want to go play there again?"

Ty swivels around to the submarine, looking torn for a moment, before the bright blue contraption seems to trump the latest game and he runs off towards it.

"Hey," Felix says, touching my arm. "I'm sorry. I didn't mean to . . ." He trails off, because really, what is he apologizing for?

For being awesome with my kid? For making him happy in this way I'm not sure I can?

"Don't apologize," I say, shaking my head. "I really like seeing you be so good with him. I kind of love it, actually." I reach out and touch his waist, running my hand along the cotton of his Johnny Cash t-shirt.

"Really?" He looks a little dubious.

"Yes," I say, and it's true. "It's just that—it's stupid, I know, but I see how good you are with him, just like naturally, and . . ." I feel a burning behind my eyes, and blink quickly. "I'm just not.

Not like you, or Rachel, or—I want to be, but every time I try, it just . . . it doesn't feel like it's enough. It doesn't feel easy, like it seems to be for everyone else. And I'm his mom, you know? So why can't I just—"

The words catch in my throat. I look away from Felix to where Ty is back at the submarine, back to turning and turning the periscope, all of it blurred in my teary vision.

Felix puts his arms around me, tugging me closer to him. "That's the problem, I think," he says. "It's because you're his mom."

I blink at him, confused, and Felix continues. "Look, it's easy for me, because no one expects me to be automatically good at this—I'm a seventeen-year-old kid, for god's sake, with no little brothers or sisters. There's no pressure for me to figure it out instantly, and it doesn't mean anything about me if I don't. It's the same thing with Rachel."

I feel myself shrinking inward. "Rachel's always been more of a mom to him than I am."

"Right. She can do that easier, because there's not even remotely the same pressure on her as there is on you. Not that there hasn't ever been any pressure, or that it's been easy on your family in general," he says quickly, when he sees me start to object. "But she *isn't* his mom. You are. You became a mom when you were way too young for that kind of responsibility. But you're still his mom, and because of that, you can't help but feel that whether you're naturally good at this or not *means* something, like about you or about whether you'll ever be able to have a relationship with him."

The tears spill over, as his words sink in. "Doesn't it, though?"

"I don't think so, Jenna. I really don't." He presses his forehead against mine. "It's bound to make you scared, though. And that's hard to get past. But you *are* good with him. And you love him."

I've never told Felix that; I rarely let myself even think it. But I nod against his forehead, brushing away at the tears.

"And it seems like that's probably the most important factor, yeah?" he says quietly. "That and wanting to really be his mom. If you still want that."

"Yeah," I say, with a sniffle. I smile up at him. "God, Felix, how do you manage to be so smart *and* sexy?"

He laughs. "Because you have a thing for orchestra nerds, apparently." He kisses my forehead gently.

"At least one orchestra nerd in particular," I say. I shift, and the diaper bag digs painfully into my hip, reminding me. "We should probably check Ty's diaper. Though if it's full of poop, I'm not sure I'm ready for—"

I pause, as my eyes scan the submarine, not seeing Ty there anymore. I look around the rest of the playground, seeing kids darting in and around the slides, the swings, but no Ty. My heart picks up. "Ty?"

Felix follows my anxious gaze, his arms dropping from around me, as he looks around. "Where did he go?" His voice is laced with the fear starting to pulse through my veins. "Shit."

A mom walking by holding the hand of a little girl glares at him, and he winces.

"Ty! Ty!" I call again, jogging towards the submarine, wondering if he's hidden somewhere behind the plastic front. But no, the only kid there is a beefy dark-haired boy who looks up at me with wide brown eyes.

"Do you think he ran off to the baseball field?" Felix asks. "Or the parking lot?"

Could he have made it to either of those in that short a time? How short *was* it, really? Was it longer than I'd thought, when I was so wrapped up in my own angst over Ty that I stopped doing the one thing I was here to do, which was to keep him safe?

God, how could I have lost my *son*?

As if on cue, the robot baby starts crying from inside of Felix's backpack, but we both completely ignore it. Who cares about a stupid grade when we're missing an actual child?

Panic is full-on flooding through me, and I'm about to start running toward the parking lot, or maybe call my mom or even 911, when a thought hits me.

"Small spaces," I murmur, and Felix blinks at me.

"What?"

"He loves to squeeze himself into small spaces," I say. "He hides under the couch, or in the Tupperware cabinet, that kind of thing." I look back at the playground with new eyes, and catch a hint of red, like his sneakers, poking out from underneath the stairs leading up to the slide. I break into a run, weaving through little kids, and Felix follows.

"Ty!" I say, dropping to my knees to see behind the stairs. Most of it is blocked off by a plastic climbing wall, so I can fit my head through, but not much more.

But that's enough. I see Ty, scrunched up underneath the stairs, his blond wispy hair plastered to his head and a big smile on his face. "Smoosh! I smoosh!"

I let out a breath so full of relief I'm dizzy with it. "Yeah, Ty. You're smooshed, all right. Come on out."

His brow furrows again. "No, I smoosh."

"I know," I say, noting even through my relief that this tiny space reeks of urine, and his pants appear to be soaked. I guess Mom knew what she was doing with that extra change of clothes. "But we need to change your diaper. And get you home."

"No!" His face is starting to get red, and my heartbeat picks up again. He's about to start throwing a tantrum. I've always gotten away quick whenever he does this, having no idea what to do for a toddler tantrum, and especially not a Ty tantrum.

And I know then that Felix is right. I'm his mom, and me not knowing what the hell I'm doing feels like it means something.

I'm not sure yet that I can completely believe it doesn't.

"How about a snack?" I try, and his lip quivers, but he doesn't start screaming, so I take that as a good sign. "You want a snack, Ty?"

He nods, and starts to climb out, and the minute he's free,

I have the urge to grab him and hug him, pee and all, because I'm so happy he's okay.

But I don't, because I'm also afraid he'll start screaming and pull away from me, and I'm not sure I can handle that right now.

"You found him," Felix says, smiling at me. He's got the robot baby, patting it to finally shut it up. "Good job."

I smile back, but it's shaky. There's part of me that feels a little proud that I knew this thing about Ty that helped us find him.

But really I shouldn't have lost him in the first place.

Felix digs out the snacks. While Ty munches on pretzels, I change his diaper and pants while Felix shields us from anyone who might want to yell at us that you aren't supposed to change diapers on public playgrounds—is that a thing? It probably is a thing.

But it's already getting close to dinner time, and even the snack and a few more rounds of Super Ty don't keep him from melting down when we tell him it's time to go home, and Ty sobs and screams all the way back home. My mom tries to make me feel better about it—"Oh, he hates leaving the park, I should have warned you," she says, like a dozen times. And I know that's probably true. It's not like I don't hear him scream like this for her or Dad sometimes, or for Rachel.

But I can't help but feel relieved again when Felix and I drop him off at my house and leave, just the two of us and our robot baby.

And I hate myself for it.

THIRTEEN

Jenna

The next morning I wake up to the sound of Felix's phone alarm. He reaches out to turn it off, and I roll over drowsily in bed, fitting myself even more closely against his chest, breathing him in, enjoying his warmth.

He makes a satisfied sound as he tightens his arms back around me, and I feel his lips against my hair.

I want to stay here forever with him, and I think he wouldn't mind it either. But there was a reason he set his alarm an hour earlier than usual.

I let out a sigh and nudge him in the side. "You need to practice."

"I do," he groans. But he just runs his hand down my bare back, his fingers stroking along the curve of my ass.

"Mmmm," I say, smiling against his neck. "I think we practiced *that* last night."

And we did at that, all of my stress and nerves from our day at the park vanished in the need and searing heat of Felix and I clinging together, making love. *Being* in love.

"Maybe I'm a perfectionist," he says.

I laugh. "I think you are. And that's why I'm going to force you out of bed, against my own self-interest, to play your cello.

And later today, we can get back to this practice." I let my hands roam south of his waist and he groans again. "Though I think we're already pretty perfect at it."

"That's the truth." He tugs me in close for a kiss, and then reluctantly drags himself out of bed and into the shower, while I enjoy a few more luxurious minutes of dozing in the warmth of his bed.

After getting dressed, he goes to the sunroom to play, and though I want to come join him—and spend some quality time with that grand piano—I take a quick shower myself first, to give him some time to play on his own. I brought my clothes and makeup this time, so we wouldn't have to go back to my house before school again, and it takes me only a few minutes to change and pin my wet hair up into my standard buns.

I'm just leaving the bathroom, steam trailing out behind me, when the baby starts crying. I pick up the doll from the nightstand—where we could reach it easily in the night to shut it up—and pat it, feeling the soft cotton of Ty's pajamas. I'll have to remember to take those off before we turn in our doll. Today is the last day of Felix and my joint-parenting venture.

Of a robot child, at least.

Is it possible that one day we might really be parenting together?

The baby's wails die down, until all I can hear are the low, soft notes of Felix's cello from the main floor, and I start to smile at the sound—

Until I turn and see the woman standing in the open doorway, watching me. Tall and slim and impeccably dressed in a gray pencil skirt and plum silk blouse, blond hair pulled back in a chignon, a tasteful string of white pearls around her neck. She looks like she's stepped straight out of a brochure for some fancy country club.

Felix's mom. My heart pounds unsteadily.

"I think it's well past time for a proper introduction," she says, stepping into the room. Her tone isn't exactly pleasant, it's too careful for that. More like . . . neutral. "I'm Mrs. Mays."

"Jenna," I say, weakly. She doesn't extend her hand to shake, so I don't either.

She looks me up and down, her gaze hard. She has the same blue eyes as Felix, but hers are somehow so much colder than his, even when he used to look at me with bitterness.

I shift, uncomfortably aware of how short my skirt is, how my bra straps are clearly visible under my tank top. Normally, this doesn't bother me—not in front of teachers, not in front of the principal, and sure as hell not in front of my parents. But now . . .

"Why don't you come join me for coffee in the kitchen?" she asks.

I don't get the feeling this is a request. And honestly, I'm becoming more and more aware of the tangled sheets on Felix's bed, the puddles of yesterday's clothes on the floor. The box of condoms on the nightstand.

I nod. The kitchen is better.

I quickly grab my backpack and shove my old clothes into it and the baby as well, then follow her downstairs. The sound of Felix's cello grows louder. He's playing a classical piece, and though I'm not the biggest fan of classical, it's gorgeous. Calming.

Or would be, if I wasn't being led to a coffee-chat with Felix's uber-WASP of a mother, who even he as much as admitted would hate me.

When I reach the large, magazine-pristine kitchen, she pours coffee into an oddly slender mug and hands it to me. It smells like hazelnut.

"Thank you," I say, and she gives a thin-lipped smile, and sits at the table.

"I was surprised to hear Felix had a new girlfriend," she says, taking a sip from her own mug. "I suppose I shouldn't have been. He's always been easily distracted by a pretty girl."

I'm almost disappointed in this tactic, it's such an obvious

145

one. Trying to imply that Felix is a player, and I'm just the latest piece of ass. "Distracted?" I say, trying to keep my voice as perfectly neutral as she does. "He seems pretty focused to me." I tilt my head towards the sunroom like I'm talking about his cello playing, though we both know I'm not.

Her smile gets even thinner. "Well, yes. He can be quite driven when he wants something. And nothing drives him more than his music, I'm sure you know."

"He's an incredible musician," I say carefully.

Is it my imagination, or is there actually a spark of warmth in her eyes when I say that?

"He loves that cello more than anything in the world. He always has." She lets out a small chuckle. "I never saw a child so determined to be the best at something, and that includes my daughter Dana."

I've heard plenty about Dana, and I find myself starting to smile for real at this.

Maybe I'm reading too much coldness into Felix's mom. Maybe she really does just want to talk to me, to get to know Felix's girlfriend. I take a drink of coffee, which is way better than the canned stuff we have at home. Damn.

"He'll be so happy when he's finally at Juilliard," she says.

I nearly spit out my coffee, but manage to swallow it just in time. It burns my throat on the way down.

"Juilliard?" I manage. There's no hiding my surprise.

Her perfectly groomed eyebrows lift just the smallest amount. "Why, yes. Juilliard. He hasn't told you?"

"I—um, we haven't really been together that long." I look down at the coffee mug.

Juilliard? In New York?

"Well, I'm still surprised he didn't mention it. It's been his dream since he was little—not long after he first picked up the cello, in fact. Do you know that's why he practices four hours a day? Because he learned that is required of Juilliard students and decided he wanted to be well prepared." Her French-manicured

146

nails clink against the coffee mug. "He's been putting everything he has towards this for years—right now he has a bit of a break after All-State, but he has a Young Artists competition coming up in July, and I think he has a real chance at taking the grand prize this year. He would have had it last year if the judges hadn't been so taken with that girl from Victorville with that folk-metal electric thing. But I suppose it's popular on *Twitter*." She shakes her head, like both Twitter and folk metal are somehow beneath both her and her son, though I'm not exactly sure what the second one is. "Then in the fall he's been invited to play with the Los Angeles Orchestra. It keeps him very busy, but that's what you do to achieve your dreams, don't you agree?"

"Right," I say, weakly. It doesn't surprise me that Felix is playing in more than just the school orchestra, or that he has a chance to play in adult circles. I hadn't thought about how much time he probably has to devote to playing when he's competing, and while it would be hard not to be able to see him as much, I understand. It would be worth it, to see him succeed at something he loves so much.

But Juilliard. It's the best music school in the country, and the most famous, and a student from there could probably get work in any orchestra in the world. She could be lying, I suppose, but I don't think so. Of course he'd want to go there. Of course that would be a dream for him. God, it might've been a dream for me if I hadn't given up on dreams a long time ago.

At least I thought I had, until him.

Mrs. Mays clears her throat, just the tiniest amount, getting me to look back up at her. Her blue eyes study me. "It would be a shame if, after all that work, all these years, anything jeopardized that dream for him."

My stomach twists. It's so clear what she's trying to say, and I wish she'd just fucking *say* it. "Anything?"

Her lips twist. "He's talented, of course. But Juilliard also looks at grades, which he's done well at. Though the school tells me he's been missing several classes this week, which is unusual for him."

But not unusual for me, obviously. My cheeks burn. If she called the school, she probably heard about a lot more than just missing classes. Any of the secretaries, or the principal, would have been more than happy to fill her in about me.

"And there's more than that," my mom continues. "There's letters of recommendation. We're friends at the country club with several prominent members of the Los Angeles orchestra community who would write glowing recommendations for Felix. But these people are all about appearances," she says, as if letting me in on some dirty little secret. "If they found out that Felix was involved with someone that they felt might be unworthy of young man like him, someone who might be a bad influence . . ." She gestures vaguely, as if this bad influence might be hidden somewhere in the kitchen, but she needs the maid's help to locate it, and I can't take it anymore.

"Like me, you mean."

She pauses. I'm guessing she doesn't usually deal in directness. In the background, Felix starts playing a new song, something deep and haunting. Beautiful and dark.

"You have a son yourself, is that correct?" she finally asks.

"Yes," I say. Yep, she's done her research.

She leans in a little. "You can understand my concern, then, perhaps. I'm just a mother who wants the best for her son's future—who wants him to have the future he's always wanted for himself, that he's worked so hard for. Isn't that what all mothers really want for their children?"

God, this woman couldn't twist the knife in deeper if she tried. And she's definitely trying, I know that.

But it's working anyway.

Guilt floods through me for reasons she probably hasn't even intended—have I even given much thought to Ty's future? Not really. I want him to be safe and happy, but the most effort I've given towards that goal has been to keep myself at a distance so I don't mess up his life the way I've messed up mine.

And so far, that seems to be working. Ty *is* safe and

happy—and maybe my wanting to be a bigger part of his life is pure selfishness on my part, and not motherly inclinations at all.

But what am I doing to Felix by being part of *his* life?

Mrs. Mays seems to be waiting for a response, though I get the feeling she's cataloging every expression on my face.

"Yeah, I guess so," I say.

She smiles, like we're in total agreement on everything. "Good. I just want what's in my son's best interest. And I hope you want that for him too, no matter how long this little relationship lasts." Her eyes grow even harder, little chips of blue rock. "And I think, deep down, you know it won't last long. Felix is meant for better things."

I gape a little. Okay, maybe she *can* be direct when she wants to be.

I want to tell her to go fuck herself. I want to laugh at her obvious manipulations and storm out.

But I don't, and I can't. Because even though she's being a total bitch about it, she's right.

I do know it. I always have, even if I let myself forget that these last few days. Felix deserves better than me. His future is brighter without me in it.

The problem is, I know he loves me, so he probably doesn't realize this truth himself. Is that why he didn't tell me about Juilliard? Because he knows this thing between us has a guaranteed end date and can't face that right now?

Or is it because he's starting to doubt that there should be an end date, even for something like Juilliard?

If I really love him—and I do; god, I do—then can I really let him throw away his dreams for me? This thing he's worked for all his life? Can I live with myself, knowing I dragged him down into the sucking whirlpool of my mistakes like I've done with my parents or my sister, just because I was too selfish to let him go?

Could he really be happy with me, or are we both just fooling ourselves?

Mrs. Mays stands up, brings her coffee mug to the sink. "Well, I'll go say goodbye to Felix before I go to work. But it's been lovely talking with you, Jenna."

I don't say anything back, and she doesn't seem to expect me to. She sweeps out of the kitchen with a clack of heels on Spanish tile, leaving me at the table, holding a warm cup of coffee in hands that feel ice cold. Listening to Felix's cello, the notes low and rich and breaking my heart.

FOURTEEN

Felix

Jenna is quiet on the way to school, and though she kisses me goodbye before we head our separate ways to class, she won't look me in the eye. I want to ask her what's wrong—I thought things had been going really well, and last night was hot enough I'm surprised we didn't both catch fire. I'm glad it's finally Friday, first because we can at last turn in our little robot baby, and because bright and early tomorrow morning I'm going to need to make up all that practice I missed this week.

We'll talk in health class, I tell myself. But Jenna comes in to health class late—I've still got the kid, as per our arrangement, and she almost misses our score. We got an eighty-eight percent overall—which isn't half bad considering how much we ignored the baby this week. I pay her the last of her money for the day, and she returns to her seat. On my way by, I steal the empty desk next to her.

"What are you planning to do with all that cash?" I ask. We got a ninety percent three out of five days, having failed as parents the day we lost her at Disneyland, and the day that we left her in the car and hung out with Jenna's family.

Whoops.

Jenna shrugs. "I don't know."

151

She still won't look at me.

"Jenna," I say. "What's wrong?"

She shakes her head. "Nothing." There's a long pause. Obviously something is wrong, though I can't imagine what changed this morning while I was playing—

Oh.

"Did my mom say something to you?" I ask.

"I was thinking of trying to find a used piano," Jenna says.

It takes me a moment to realize she's talking about the money. "Yeah? That seems like a good use of it." Though it occurs to me that she's also going to need a prom dress. "Do you already have a dress for prom? I was going to buy the tickets today, but honestly, the way you dress is so sexy, you don't need to get a new dress if you don't want to. I have a suit that I use to perform, so probably I'll just wear that, and—"

"Can we talk about this later?" Jenna asks.

I look up at the front of the classroom, where Angela and Daniel are getting their final scores. Under normal circumstances, I'd make a crack at Daniel about scoring, but right now I have other things to worry about. We don't have anything particular we're supposed to be working on until all the partnerships have checked in their babies.

Which I'm guessing means Jenna wants to talk where no one can hear.

"At lunch?" I ask. "We could meet at the dugout."

"Yeah," Jenna says. "That would be good."

I reach over and take her hand, earning a glare from Angela as she walks back to her desk. There's some laughter at the back of the class, and I imagine that, too, is about us.

"It'll be okay," I tell Jenna, before I head back to my seat. Though I think I may be saying that more for me than for her.

By the time I meet Jenna out by the dugout at lunch, I've figured out what must have happened. Things were fine this morning. More than fine. It wasn't until after I did my practice this morning that Jenna got quiet.

I find Jenna huddled on the bench in the dugout, her shoes on the bench, and her knees tucked up against her chest.

"My mother said something to you, didn't she?" I ask.

Jenna looks up at me. "Why didn't you tell me about Juilliard?"

"What?" I'm honestly not sure what she's talking about, but I'm even more sure my mom had something to do with it. "What about Juilliard?"

Jenna looks at me like I'm patronizing her. "That you've been planning to go there since you were a kid. It's your dream, isn't it? And you didn't even tell me about it."

"It's been a week, Jenna," I say. "I'm sure you haven't told me everything there is to know about yourself, either."

"I would have told you if I was moving to New York."

Ah. That's what this is about. "I haven't even applied," I tell her. "I don't have any immediate plans to move anywhere."

"But you'll get in," Jenna says. "You know you will."

I want to tell her that we can go to New York together, but of course we can't. Not if she wants to be a mother to Ty. Hopefully in another year she'll be more comfortable with him, but I doubt either of us will be comfortable enough that we'll want to move across the country to take care of him by ourselves. Besides, that wouldn't be fair to the kid. He needs to stay near his grandparents, since they've been the ones raising him. "I don't even know if I'm going to apply," I tell her. "And even if I do and I get in, I don't think I'm going to go."

"That's because of me, isn't it?"

"Yeah," I say. "Yeah, of course it is. I get that you can't just run off to New York, and if you can't go, I don't want to." I haven't thought through the details of this, but I'm sure we'll be able to work it out. There are plenty of schools around here. Or

I can try auditioning, and see if my skills are good enough to get work right away. There are more paying gigs in LA than there are spots for cellists at Juilliard, for sure. My parents wouldn't be happy about it, but I bet my dad would be swayed by the argument that there's no reason for me to pay to play when I could be getting paid to play just as well.

Jenna shakes her head. "You can't do that. You can't give up something like that for me."

"I want to," I say. "I want to be with you, and Juilliard isn't the only place in the world that I can play. We could play together, maybe. That would be awesome."

"I don't perform. And you're too good not to."

"I can get work here. I don't want to go to New York without you. And besides, that's more than a year away. We have plenty of time to talk about it."

Jenna's eyes go cold, and she looks down at the ground.

Oh. Oh, god. "Jenna?" I say. "We have a lot of time to talk about it, don't we?"

"I don't think we should do this," Jenna says. "I don't think we should be together."

My whole body goes cold. "What are you talking about? Of course we should be. I love you."

"No, Felix," Jenna says. "You're wasting yourself with me. You have the potential to do amazing things, and you shouldn't be stuck here with me."

"I'm not stuck," I tell her, desperate for her to understand. "I *want* to be with you. I want that more than I ever wanted to go to Juilliard."

Jenna shakes her head. She still won't look at me, and I can tell she's already decided. There's nothing I can say. My feet feel rooted to the spot, like I might never move, like I might turn into a statue, staring into this moment as the seasons change around me. We're in southern California, where we don't really have seasons, but I'm still picturing my body being buried in fall leaves and then snow, lost and forgotten.

"Don't do this to me," I say. My voice is grainy and my eyes are starting to burn. "I'm sorry about my mom, but don't give up on me like this. I didn't mean to not tell you about Juilliard. I didn't think it was relevant because I'm not even sure I want to go."

Jenna stands up, her arms folded tight around herself. "You'll get in. And you'll be happy there."

And then she brushes by me, stalking across the softball field and away from campus. I sink onto the bench, unable to breathe, unable to move, long after the lunch bell rings and I'm supposed to be back in class.

You'll be happy there, Jenna said.

But she's wrong. I'm not sure that I'll ever be happy again.

FIFTEEN

Jenna

I only go back into the school to get my backpack, because it has my phone and house keys in it. The halls are busy, students coming and going from lunch. Some notice me and look away too quickly, others stare openly, checking me out. One guy makes a gesture of sucking on his finger like a blow job and his friends laugh. There's a couple making out against their lockers the way Felix and I did yesterday.

I stare straight ahead, and try to ignore all of it. It's not hard to do, because all I can really see is Felix's expression when I told him we shouldn't be together. His blue eyes shiny with tears; the pain etched across his face. All I can hear is the thin desperation to his voice.

Don't do this to me.

Don't give up on me like this.

I love you.

I push so hard on the exit doors to the school the sound is like a crack of thunder. Or maybe that's just how I hear it, this booming of a raging storm ahead. Whipping winds and crashing rains, a downpour that could drown the whole world—or at least sweep me away entirely.

But the day outside is LA sunny and bright, and the only

storm, the only devastation, is happening entirely inside me.

And Felix, too, I think, which is so much worse.

Don't do this to me.

But the truth is, it was already long done, and neither of us knew it. I let myself believe this could happen, that someone like me could in any way fit into his life, could do anything but ultimately mess up everything he's worked so hard for. Or maybe I didn't ever really believe it, deep down. Maybe I just selfishly ignored every flicker of conscience, because I wanted to believe so, so badly.

Rachel knew. She tried to tell me, and I didn't listen. And I hurt him, just like she said I would.

I could take it all back. I could turn around and run back into the school, find him still at the dugout, maybe. Or wait by his locker for him to get out of class. Or text him to meet me.

I could tell him I'm sorry, I didn't mean it, of course we should be together, no matter what. I could take away his hurt, and mine, and it would feel so good, so perfect, so right—

I stop, just at the curb at the edge of the school parking lot, my legs trembling with the need to turn around and find Felix and make it all right again.

But Mrs Mays' voice echoes in my head.

He'll be so happy when he's finally at Juilliard.

He's been putting everything he has towards this for years.

Felix didn't deny that he'd been planning to go before he met me. He didn't even deny it had been his dream to do so, before me. I'm guessing his mom was telling the truth about his insane four hour a day practice schedule—all leading him towards Juilliard, towards playing with and learning from the best cellists in the world.

If I could go to New York next year, maybe . . .

I can almost picture it, us in New York. Sharing some crappy apartment, eating big slices of pizza at 2 AM. Walking hand-in-hand down busy sidewalks slick with snow, our breath misting out in front of us as we make each other laugh, the night lit up around us with city lights. Him going to school during the day, and me doing . . . I don't know. Something. Waitressing, or working retail somewhere.

Us playing music together in the evenings. Waking up together in the mornings.

But Ty. I can't leave Ty like that; I know it on some bone-deep level. Even if I fail over and over again at being his mom, even if I give up and keep the level of being in his life I've managed so far, I can't leave him and move across the country. I can tell Felix knows that.

He says he would rather be with me now, that even if he made it in to Juilliard—which he would, I know he would, a person can't have heard him play and think otherwise—he probably wouldn't go. And even as that knowledge that he would give something like that up for me—*me*, after only a few days of being together—makes me feel more loved than I'd been able to imagine possible before this week, I also know I can't do that to him.

I can't take away his dream, can't jeopardize his future when I have so little to offer in its place.

Just me. Just my messed-up life and my issues and, okay, some intensely great sex.

And love. He has that, has my whole heart. But the best way I know how to show it is to not be selfish. To let him hurt now to save him from even more hurt later. When he realizes that what he gained isn't worth what he lost.

He would resent me, eventually, if he stayed. He would regret throwing away his future. Thinking of that makes my heart, already cracked all to hell, feel like it's splintering into little shards.

My feet start moving again, away from the school. Back on the long walk towards home. Cars occasionally honk their horns at me, a couple guys wolf-whistle at me, but I barely hear them. Tears run down my cheeks, but I barely feel them. It takes me over an hour, and my feet, in heeled boots not made for any kind of long-distance trekking, are killing me, but the pain is nothing. Welcome, even, because with each biting step I know I deserve it for that destroyed look on his face. Deserve it for letting myself believe it could end any other way.

When I get home, I'm glad to see the house is empty. Dad's at work, and Mom and Ty are gone somewhere—maybe they got a friend to drive them to that park he loves, and he's playing in a plastic submarine. Maybe he's asking for "Fee-yix" because he wants to be Super Ty again.

Maybe I hurt him, too. Again, and always.

I walk through the empty house, past the spot in the living room where the piano used to be and now just has a toy box and a small crate of Ty's books. On an afternoon like this, alone in the house, I used to play and play. Whatever pain I felt, whatever hurt and loss and terrifying bits of guarded hope, I would pour into my music.

This, though . . . this is pain I don't think music can hold, even if I had a piano to play on.

I think of the cash in my backpack, of my plans to get a used piano. Of my thought that maybe someday Felix and I could play together at my house—it wouldn't be a grand piano, or anything close, but it would be even better, because it was ours. His and mine, even though he would never claim that. I'd earned it, he'd say. With my negotiation skills and my excellent robot baby parenting.

But it would always be his, too, in my mind. Not just the piano, even. The music, too.

The splinters of my heart ache so much it hurts to breathe.

I go upstairs and I toss my backpack to the corner of the room where it lands in a pile of laundry. Then I slump at the foot of my bed and hold my knees to my chest and sit there, trembling and remembering every moment of every day this week with Felix. Every touch of his hand in mine, every kiss, every time he smiled at me in that way that made me feel, for the first time maybe ever, really alive.

I don't know how long I sit there before the dam breaks and I start sobbing. And I really don't know how long I cry—deep, wracking, gulping sobs that shake my whole body. But at some point my door opens, and a hesitant voice breaks through my grief.

"Jenna?"

It's Rachel. I want to tell her to go away, but I can't speak. I can't tell another person I love to go away right now. Not again.

I stay huddled down, my face against my knees, and I feel her sit down next to me. There's a pause, and then she says. "I'm sorry, Jenna. Whatever happened, I'm sorry."

"Me too," I manage, my throat raw with grief.

I feel my sister's arm around my shoulders, pulling me towards her, and it shakes loose another round of sobs. She just holds me and I cry until I can't cry anymore. And then she holds me some more, as we just sit there. She doesn't ask me to explain, and I don't offer. But if I could, it would be this:

It was inevitable I would hurt him. I'm Jenna Rollins; it's what I do. I hurt people.

But I hope that this time, I'm doing the right thing. At least for him.

SIXTEEN

Felix

I wake up hours later, buried under blankets on my bed. It's a warm spring day and my house is climate-controlled as ever, sixty-nine degrees all year round. But my body is freezing, like I've just come in out of the snow, and I think part of my soul is still out there at the softball field.

Maybe it always will be.

I close my eyes. I just want to go to sleep and never wake up, but my brain won't oblige. My fingers crawl over the empty space beside me. I know I was spoiled, being able to bring my girlfriend home with me to spend the night, but I still ache without her here.

She's gone. I feel like I held the most beautiful thing in the world in the palm of my hand, and then a wind picked up and blew it away.

No, not the wind.

My mother.

I look over at the clock. It's after eight, late enough that my parents are probably home.

I don't want to see them. I don't want to see anyone. But this dead emptiness inside me is howling to get out. So I get out of bed and storm downstairs.

My parents are in the kitchen, my father scrolling on his phone, my mother with the latest real estate offerings up on the screen of her laptop. She looks up at me, takes a sip of her tea, and smiles. "Felix, honey," she says. "I saw you were asleep. Are you feeling well?"

"What did you say to Jenna?" I ask.

My mother's eyebrows go up, in a look of feigned innocence. "Jenna? Is that your girlfriend's name? I was just chatting with her this morning. She's certainly an interesting girl."

My dad puts down his phone. "I just met her yesterday. I think 'interesting' is a good word for it."

"What did you *say* to her?" I ask again.

My mother now pretends to be confused. "We just chatted about you. That clearly being the only thing we have in common. I don't know what you mean."

"Jenna broke up with me," I say. "Because of whatever you said. That I'm going to go to Juilliard, maybe? And abandon her?"

My mom blinks like this is stunning news. She really should have been an actress instead of a real estate agent. She could win an Oscar for this performance. "Were you keeping that a secret from her?" she says. "I would have thought that since you two were so close, she'd have known about your future plans."

I grit my teeth. That statement is a trap, and it's activated land mines all around me. I can't say that I didn't tell Jenna, because then it's my fault for deceiving her. I can't address the implication that she's pissed at me for having my girlfriend spend the night, because it's veiled, and she'll only deny it. I can't say I'm not going to Juilliard, because then my parents' heads will explode, along with the shattered remains of what used to be my life.

But at this moment, fire sounds better than ice.

"I don't even know if I'm going to Juilliard," I say. "I haven't made any decisions yet about my future."

My mother looks horrified, and my father pushes his chair back from the table. "Felix," Dad says. "Of course you're going.

You'll get in. I'm sure of it."

I take a step back. "Maybe I don't want to go to New York. You've been talking about Juilliard since I was eleven. I'm seventeen now, and maybe that's not what I want anymore. Maybe I like it in LA, and I'm going to stay here."

My mother purses her lips. "Felix, you certainly can't make these kinds of decisions because of a *girl*."

I should tell them that it's not Jenna. I should tell them this is what I want. And it is, but the fact is I'm not sure I ever would have figured it out without her. I was dead inside, working so hard to get to the only place anyone had ever thought I could belong, hoping when I got there I could finally be happy. And then Jenna came along and breathed life into my everyday existence, filling my life with magic.

"Let's not make any decisions about your future today," Dad says. "You'll apply to Juilliard, do your audition, and then we'll see."

"I'm not going," I say. It feels so *good* to say those words. I'm not going to Juilliard. I'm not going to commit myself to another four years of no one giving a damn about anything about me besides the way I play. I'm not going to get pushed into it, just because I happen to be good, just because my parents have decided that's what I'm going to do.

Because I already know I'm not going to belong there. I found the place where I belonged. With *her*.

"Honey," my mother says harshly. "Of course you are. You can't jeopardize your whole future over a high school crush. And especially not over a girl like *that*."

"A girl like *what*?" I ask.

My mother goes back to her look of feigned innocence. Even my father seems interested to know what she's going to say. I should be glad that they're not secretly conspiring to drive Jenna out of my life, but I'm not. It doesn't matter. In the end, my dad is going to agree with my mom, no matter what she does.

"Felix," she says. "You must be aware that Jenna has something of a reputation."

"Yeah," I say. "I bet I know more about it than you do."

"And you know that she has a *child*," Mom says.

Ah yes. It took her less than a day to discover all kinds of reasons not to want me dating Jenna. The parental gossip chain at its finest.

"Yeah, I do," I say. "And he's adorable. I don't see what that has to do with—"

"Felix," my dad says, in a voice like he's trying to calm a startled animal. "You can't possibly think you're ready to be a father."

"Are *you*? Because Mom just destroyed the only good thing to happen to me in as long as I can remember."

Dad blinks at me.

"*Felix*," Mom says. "Don't talk to your father that way."

"Why not?" I ask.

I hear footsteps out in the hall. Our conversation must have gotten loud enough to attract Gabby. She's wisely staying outside for the moment—she hates arguments and usually stays as far away from them as possible.

"Because we're your parents," my mother says. "And if you can't see why shacking up with a girl like that might put your future in danger . . . just think about what would happen if the people at Juilliard found out."

"First," I say, "the people at Juilliard are not going to care who I'm sleeping with."

"*Felix*." Mom clutches her hand to her chest like I've said something truly shocking, even though she just intimated I was having sex with Jenna the sentence before.

"And second," I say, "I don't care what they say, because I'm not applying to Juilliard. I'm not going to New York, and you can't make me. You can fill out the application for me, but you can't make me audition. And I won't, Mom. There's nothing you can do about it."

"Felix," my father says. "Go to your room."

I laugh at that. It's bitter and humorless, but still. The idea that they think they can send me to my room like I'm a little kid because I say I won't apply to the college they've decided I should go to . . . "Why? So you don't have to talk to me anymore?"

"So you can think about what kind of an influence this girl has clearly had on you," Dad says. "Talking about throwing away your future? I've certainly never heard anything like it from my son."

"No, you haven't," I say. "Because you've never asked me what I want. You've never taken two seconds to consider that maybe I should be the one to decide what I'm going to do with the rest of my life. And that maybe it shouldn't be motivated by what looks best for you."

"Felix," Mom says. "Your father told you to go to your room."

I look between the two of them. I want to yell at them, but it won't do any good. This isn't a conversation. I'm talking to a wall. And it's true what I told Jenna. Neither of them gives a shit about me. They want to lock me up in a box labeled "teenage rebellion" and open it once I'm ready to toe the line.

"I'll do one better. I'm out of here." I stalk down the hall toward the front door, pulling my keys out of my pocket. I pass Gabby in the hall without looking at her, and she follows after me. I look back once. Neither of my parents are following.

"Felix," Gabby says. "What happened?"

"Mom told Jenna I was going to abandon her to go to New York," I say. "And probably some other stuff about how she was jeopardizing my future, and she needed to break up with me so that I could achieve my wondrous potential." I throw open the front door and storm out onto the driveway, Gabby right on my heels.

"Oh my god, Felix," she says. "I'm sorry."

"Yeah. Me too." But sorry isn't going to change the look on Jenna's face when she told me she didn't want me anymore. Sorry isn't going to change that I finally found someone I loved, someone who made me feel alive and strong and good about myself.

And then Mom had to take her away.

"They don't care," I say. "They don't care about anything they can't brag about to their friends. I'm going to disappear, and they don't fucking care."

Gabby puts a hand on my shoulder, but I stalk away. I know I'm not being fair to her. Mom and Dad are way worse to her than they are to me, always treating her like she's some kind of screw-up just because she doesn't have some genius talent they can rely on to make her distinguished and award-winning and worth something.

The fact is, she does. Gabby is the most deeply good person I've ever known, and she loves people fiercely. And while no one is handing out any awards for this, it's definitely the reason she follows me to my car, even though I don't want her to.

I unlock the car and open the door.

"Felix," Gabby says, "where are you going to go?"

"I'm going to find a party. And get wasted." I can't bear to be inside my own mind right now. I can't bear to inhabit my own body. I have to get out, and short of killing myself, this is the only way I can think of to escape.

"You can't do that," Gabby says. "You're underage."

I give her a look, and she holds up her hands. "Okay, okay, so technically you *can* do that. But you shouldn't. And where are you even going to find a party anyway?"

"It's Friday night in Los Angeles. I don't think it'll be a problem." I get into the driver's seat and slam the door, but Gabby hauls open the passenger side and climbs in beside me.

I glare at her. "Gabby, get out."

She's frantic. "And how do you think you're going to get home? Are you going to drive home wasted?"

"Maybe," I say, even though I know that's a terrible idea.

"I am not letting you drive drunk. I'm your designated driver."

"You don't want to watch this," I say. "I'm going to get drunk, and maybe do drugs, too. I don't know."

God, I sound like an idiot. I wouldn't even know how to find drugs. But Jenna seems to manage, and right now all I want is to power down, to shut my brain off and leave it that way for as long as humanly possible.

"Felix," Gabby says, "I know you're hurting. But you don't want to do this."

"Actually, I do." I put my car in reverse and back out of our long driveway, and Gabby buckles up for the ride.

I'm going to find a party, and I'm going to listen to loud music and drink myself into oblivion. That's what Jenna's probably doing right now, and it seems to work just fine for her.

SEVENTEEN

Jenna

Hours later, I'm still huddled in that same spot, now by myself. A hollow shell, cried out. Rachel tried to bring me a plate of dinner I didn't eat. My mom knocked on the door, said my name, but I didn't answer and she didn't pry. I've trained them all pretty well to leave me alone.

A text dings on my phone, and there's the faintest jolt of hope that it's Felix. Still in love with me, maybe, even after I've hurt him. Not that it would change anything. Not that it would make me someone who could be good for him.

But the text is from Ian. Of course, it's Friday night. We go out to parties during the week fairly often, but Fridays and Saturdays are pretty much a constant.

Should I get you? Or are you ditching me for your boyfriend?
I blink at it.

I don't have a boyfriend anymore. Such a huge loss, such a soul-gutting emptiness left behind, for something I only had for mere days.

I don't want to move. But also, I don't want to feel this pain, this raging storm that, even after all that crying, is still there, battering me from the inside out.

And I know things that can make the pain go away, at least

for a little while.

Plus, I'm Jenna Rollins. This is what I do.

I text Ian back, my fingers numb.

Come get me.

His reply is immediate.

Be there in 10.

I push myself to my feet, which sends sharp pains through me from all the blisters I undoubtedly got on my long walk home. I'm still wearing those god-awful shoes, but whatever. It's too much effort to change. I look at myself in the mirror, and am not surprised that I look like total hell. I'm red-faced and blotchy, like I've already spent the afternoon pounding back shots. Mascara is streaked down my cheeks. Hair juts out even more strangely than normal from the buns I keep it in.

I consider just going like this. Ian wouldn't care, nor would anyone else at the party.

No one would care, because no one ever does.

But ultimately I decide to at least wipe the mascara off my cheeks so I don't look like a goth zombie. I re-pin my hair. I swipe on lipstick, a stain of cherry red. My clothes from school—short black skirt with tiny white skulls across it like polka dots, a tight-fitting black tank top, lace-up boots, stacked silver rings—are party-ready.

I don't look great, but it doesn't really matter. I'm good enough for *this*. It may be the only thing I've been good enough for.

Ian's car horn sounds, as usual. He's no gentleman caller, to come to my front door and meet my parents. They'd hate him anyway, even if they knew he was just my friend and barely even that.

Not like Felix, who they loved, even though they had no idea why he'd be with me.

It's probably the only thing I've agreed with them on in years.

I grab my purse and my phone and leave the room. I pass by Ty's room on the way out, see his door cracked open. He'll

169

be asleep now, and there's this tug I feel to go inside, to hear to his soft breathing. To see his peaceful little face in the soft glow of the night light.

I shove that thought aside. I'd probably just wake him up, and then what?

I walk out of the house, past my mom and dad, who turn from the TV show they're watching and see me go, but have long since learned it doesn't stop me to say anything. Past Rachel, who sits curled up in the armchair reading that book from her and Felix's English class, and doesn't look up at all.

Ian's crappy late-90's Dodge Neon is idling loudly out in front of my house. He could probably afford a better car, given his dealings, but he likes his own product too much, and doesn't give a shit about what he drives. I climb in and kick aside an In-N-Out bag, probably from his last late-night bout of munchies.

"Hey," he says.

"Hey," I respond.

We drive in mostly silence to whatever party he's tracked down, which is pretty typical. I think we might make it all the way there without another spoken syllable, but we're pulling into an old, cracked-asphalt neighborhood we hit up often for parties when Ian says, "So no preppy boyfriend tonight?"

My gut twists miserably. "Nope." I look out the window.

Ian pauses. "You okay?"

"I'm here, aren't I?"

He nods like I answered the question, and maybe I did. But I'm guessing the answer he heard and the one I meant were two totally different things. He parks the car at a curb near a gathering of other, likewise crappy cars, and we make our way to the ranch-style house with decorative bars over the windows and a couple of teens not-so-discreetly shooting up on the porch.

Music is thumping inside the house, but not as loudly as it would be at a frat party. Parties in neighborhoods not dotted with fraternity houses tend to be quieter, the lights dimmer and less flashy, so as not to piss off neighbors who are itchier to call the cops with complaints.

It doesn't mean there's less drugs or sex happening at these parties. There's fewer frat boys showing off stupid keg tricks, but more hardcore users. Fewer games as preamble for sex or getting wasted, most getting straight to the point. A slightly different atmosphere, but it's all about the same, as far as I'm concerned.

People here to use and be used.

I stand there just inside the house, taking it all in, in a way I rarely—if ever—bother to, like I'm watching it all from a distance, or through a TV screen. People dancing up against each other, people laughing raucously while drinking shots and beer, quieter people in darker corners snorting coke or shooting up. People making out on the threadbare couch, or getting a blow job behind it.

A few guys notice me, check me out. Smiles curve their lips. One guy, probably somewhere in his mid-twenties, with a short beard and pierced eyebrow, raises a shot to me.

Normally, that's all it would take. Normally, I'd go over to this guy and down that shot. We'd dance a bit, maybe, or not. I'd drink more and more. Maybe take a pill, if he offers. Then go with him somewhere for a quick fuck, if I'm up for it, which I usually am.

Feel wanted, for a few minutes at least. Feel numb, which is really the end-goal here, of all of it—the sex, the pills, the drinking.

But instead of being appealing, the thought of all that makes me sick. I ignore the guy and grab a beer from a cooler by the door. Then I go sit on the stairs, toying with the beer bottle.

Ian, who usually has long-since left my side by this point, follows me.

"What the hell's wrong with you?" Ian asks, and I notice I'm scowling.

I try to relax my expression. "Nothing. I guess I'm in a weird mood."

171

"Because of Felix." Ian frowns. "Did he make you feel bad about partying or something?"

I glare at him. "Shouldn't your face be planted in some girl's tits by now?"

He sighs. "Okay, sure, whatever. Just don't let him make you into something you're not, you know? You're a cool party girl, not some prissy good girl with a stick up her ass."

I don't say anything, and Ian walks away, shaking his head.

I know I'm not some prissy good girl. Not that Felix wanted me to be. But right now, I don't feel like cool party girl, either. I think of the way Felix said my name, the way he breathed it while holding my face so close to his.

He just wanted me to be *me*. Jenna.

And when I was with him, that's who I wanted to be too.

The music pulses in my veins, and even though it's not all that loud, throbs behind my temples. I take a sip of beer, but mostly just pick at the label with my fingernail.

A guy sits next to me—the same guy from before. "Hey, you're looking lonely."

"Yeah?" I say, taking another drink. I avoid meeting his eyes.

"Yeah," he says, scooting closer. "But I think I can help out with that." He puts a hand on my bare leg, just below my skirt, and I think of Felix's hand on my leg in the car, of the way it felt when his fingers inched up.

This feels nothing like that. A sweaty palm pressed too hard into my skin, like he's claiming me, and I already know what kind of sex this guy is into. The kind of stuff he'll want me to do.

My blood feels cold and sluggish, and my skin crawls under his touch. "Not interested," I say, shifting my leg away.

But he doesn't listen. "I can make you very interested," he says in what he clearly hopes is a sexy tone, leaning closer, his hand reaching up under my skirt.

My whole body cramps up with revulsion, and I jump to my feet, shoving him back. Beer sloshes out of the bottle and onto his leg, and he swears.

"Get. The fuck. Away." I say, and several people nearby turn to look at us.

"Bitch," he mutters, and stalks off.

I'm trembling as I sit back down, pressed against the stair railing like I can make myself invisible.

What am I doing here?

What have I *ever* been doing here?

Trying to make myself numb. Trying to make myself feel alive. Wanting both at the same time, and never really getting either.

But I think the truth is, I just wanted to feel something *real*. I wanted to feel seen and loved, and I looked for it in places like this, with asshole guys like this.

I had all that with Felix. Everything I've been looking for all along, everything I was afraid to even believe was possible. And I gave it up. For him, sure. But all the good intentions in the world don't make the loss any less of a gaping wound that I don't think will ever heal.

The smoke in the air—cigarette smoke mingled with weed mingled with god knows what—makes everything seem a little hazy, the laughter and voices fake and wrong. The moans of pleasure from the couple humping against the hallway wall sound distorted and empty. It all makes me want to vomit, and I've barely had half a beer.

I shouldn't be here. I don't want to be here. I stand up, my legs shaking, and head to the door, not knowing where exactly I'm going.

I can't be with Felix, but I don't want this in his place.

Not tonight, and maybe not ever again.

EIGHTEEN

Felix

It's not that hard to find fraternity row at the nearest state college, and even less hard to find a party. What is hard to find is parking; Gabby and I circle and circle throughout the surrounding neighborhoods, looking for a place that isn't taken or marked with an angry No Parking sign.

I guess they have this problem in this neighborhood a lot.

"Maybe this is a sign, Felix," Gabby says. "A sign you shouldn't be here."

"No, *Gabby*. It's a sign a lot of people in LA want to party on a Friday night." And that LA doesn't have nearly enough parking to accommodate them.

We finally find a spot three blocks away, on the fenced side of a corner lot, so hopefully the residents won't notice us. There's not technically a No Parking sign, but I imagine these guys see a lot of drunk people dragging their sorry asses back to their cars in the early and not-so-early hours of the morning.

This time, I'm going to be one of them.

I'm jittering a little as we walk up the blocks to the main row of houses. I've been to plenty of parties, but those were all with high school kids. College seems more hardcore for some reason, more dangerous. I'm always the designated driver, the guy who has one beer at the beginning of the night and then drives everyone home hours later. I've watched my friends get trashed and vomit into bushes and generally humiliate themselves, and never once have I wanted to join them.

Now, though, I just want to disappear. I don't want a party with my friends; I want something big and anonymous that I can disappear into, where no one knows or cares who I am. Gabby is putting a wrench in that, following along after me like I'm some runaway kid who just needs to outrun his own tantrum, but needs to be watched over so he doesn't get hit by a car in the meantime.

Maybe that is who I am right now, but I don't care. I'm going to get wasted and maybe high and try to forget for a moment that I'm Felix fucking Mays, who isn't good for anything except playing music and never will be. Jenna comes to these things for the hook-ups, but that's the last thing I'm interested in. All I want is a quiet corner to die in.

We walk up to a house with a bunch of Greek symbols painted on the windows, just as three guys burst out of it, laughing loudly and sloshing beer onto the street. The bass is thumping so loud the rest of the music is inaudible, and no one stops us as we walk through the front doors. All throughout the house people are dancing or making out or playing beer pong in a side room. It's too early in the night for people to be crazy wasted, but other than a couple of girls who look me over, no one seems to notice or care that we're here.

I move through the house to avoid looking awkward and drawing attention. In the kitchen I find the keg, which is manned by a couple of guys who seem to be handing cups to anyone who wants one. I grab one for me and then when Gabby doesn't immediately volunteer to take one herself, thrust one into her hands.

"Try to blend in," I say to her, as I take off through the house again.

I don't know who I'm kidding. Gabby and I are the last

people who can blend in at a party like this, though most people don't seem to care enough to notice. The bass pounds in my head like a heartbeat, and I move through the main living area, where a guy and a girl with long black hair are tearing each other's clothes off on their way up the stairs. My heart lurches up into my throat. For a moment, it's Jenna and some other guy, some guy who doesn't even care about her or know her name, who wants her to perform like some girl in a porno, who'll give her pills, do god knows what with her and then leave her unconscious for someone else to have seconds.

It's not Jenna, of course. This girl has a tattoo winding up her shoulder, sharper features and a piercing in her nose. But that only barely takes the edge off. It's Friday night, and somewhere in this city, Jenna is at a party doing exactly that.

Even worse, I'm not there to make sure she's okay.

I down the rest of my beer and go back for more.

"Felix," Gabby says.

I wheel around on her. "If you're going to harass me all night, just go home," I tell her. "Or at least go back to the car. I don't need a babysitter, and I don't need a shadow."

"You need to talk about it. Let's go outside and sit down somewhere and—"

"There's nothing to say!" I yell at her. "Go to hell, Gabby. Just go to hell."

I turn around, stalk into the kitchen and grab myself another beer, down it, and grab a third. When I look behind me, Gabby isn't following.

I didn't realize how alone I'd feel without her until she's not there. The walls seem to squeeze in on me. My head is starting to buzz from the beer, and the last thing I want to do is socialize. I head from the kitchen down into the basement, where the lighting is darker and the conversations are closer. I'm pretty sure Gabby didn't entirely leave me here, but I don't know if she'll be able to find me down here and I'm not sure if I want her to.

"Hey," a girl says to me, coming up and offering me a drink. I take it, even though I haven't finished my beer, and lean against the wall. She's still hanging close by, toying with her long blond braid, leaning up against the wall next to me where I can smell her perfume. It's too strong, stronger than the smell of the beer, and her presence is generally offensive on account of her being not Jenna. I finish both my drinks as fast as I can, and avoid eye contact.

I'm usually pretty good with girls, but this one is clearly noticing that there's something off about me. She takes a step back and then wanders away. My head is starting to spin, and I'm starting to see Jenna everywhere, getting up on this guy, or that one, throwing shade at me from the far side of the room, like I'm some kid who doesn't belong here, and she's not wrong. I stumble into the next room, looking for somewhere to sit down.

I collapse on a couch. There are some people moaning next to me and they might be having sex, or just heavily making out, and the pulse of the music is pounding in my brain. I'd worry I've wandered into a bedroom, but there are some people sitting by my feet, and I'm vaguely aware of one of them passing me something metal, something with vapor coming out of one end of it.

"He's wasted," one of them says.

And to prove that I'm not, I put my mouth over the end of the pipe and breathe in. The air is hot and sticky, like the inside of a sauna, and I relax back onto the couch and let whatever's in it claim me.

Even then, the pain doesn't stop.

NINETEEN

Jenna

I'm outside on the sidewalk several houses down from the party house before I feel like I can breathe again. The street is dark, the closest streetlight broken, and I can hear the music from the party only faintly, the voices fainter still.

I'm not going back there, but I'm too far from home to walk, especially with my feet already killing from my previous walk today. It's too early to catch a ride home from someone at the party, and though I recognized plenty of faces there—and have probably had sex with several of the guys there in the past—it's not like I know any of them. I could call a cab, but I'm short on funds, and I left the cash from Felix in my backpack.

Felix would come get me if I called him, I know. He wouldn't want me left here alone, in a neighborhood like this. But I can't ask that of him, not after I hurt him like I did. I can't call him, even though I'm desperate to hear his voice again. Even though I want more than anything to curl up in his arms and feel safe and loved again.

So who, then? I don't have any friends but Ian, not really. And my family—

My family. I swallow past the jagged feeling in my throat. No matter how tight money got, no matter how much trouble

I got into, my parents never threatened to take away my phone. They always wanted to make sure I could call them if I needed help, even though I never once did in all these years. It's not like I've never been stranded at a party like this before—I just always found some other way back, even if it meant sleeping with some random guy to get a ride.

This always seemed preferable to calling my parents, to letting them see me drunk or high or just awakened in some frat guy's room with no memory of who I was with or where those bruises on my wrists or thighs came from.

But tonight I haven't done any of those things.

Would it be so terrible to ask them for help tonight?

I dig my phone out of my purse before I lose my courage—which is kind crazy to need just to call my dad and ask for a ride home, I know, but that's the way it is.

And when I see the two missed calls on my phone, my heart skips several beats.

Felix. Felix tried to call me twice in the last five minutes.

To ask me to change my mind about us? To get a better explanation of why I can't?

My eyes burn with tears that should have long since been all cried out. I don't have any better way to tell him that he deserves more than I can give him, and I'm afraid if I try, I won't be able to let him go again.

No, I can't call him back. I can't—

A text pops up, from Felix. But it's not Felix, apparently

Jenna, this is Gabby. I got Felix's phone. We're at this frat party, and he was really upset and he took some drugs, but I don't know what kind and I'm really worried about him. Is there any way you can help me get him back home? I hate to ask you this, but I don't know who else to call.

My stomach lurches. Felix is doing *drugs*? At a *frat party*? With his *sister*?

Having someone there with him is good, in theory, if they can watch out for him. And it seems like Gabby's trying to. But what the hell is happening? Felix doesn't do drugs. Felix barely drinks.

Except maybe when he's hurting so much he doesn't know what else to do to make it stop—a feeling I'm all too familiar with. I remember the look on his face again, all but begging me not to break up with him. I close my eyes, trying to shut down the guilt and pain that still floods through me, even though I should long since have drowned in it.

What kind of drugs is he doing? Pot? Maybe some E? I'm not sure if Gabby would freak about that stuff or not.

Would he even know what he was taking if someone gave him harder stuff? Gabby clearly doesn't.

I hit the call back button, trying to tamp down the rising fear.

She picks up after a single ring, like she's been staring at the phone, willing me to call back. "Jenna?" she yells, and I wince and pull the phone away from my face. Club music is blaring from the background and the sounds of people cheering, probably from beer pong or something.

"Gabby," I say. "What's going on? Is Felix—?"

"Jenna!" She shouts again, cutting me off. "I can't hear you, it's so loud! But I don't want to go outside, I'm afraid if I don't keep an eye on him, he'll do some more—" Her words cut off at another cheer, and someone drunkenly yelling the name "Casey!" so close to the phone I wonder if he thinks Gabby is on the phone with this person.

"Gabby!" I shout back. "What is Felix doing right now? What did he—"

"Jenna! Jenna, I can't really hear you, but—oh no, they're passing it around again! He's smoking something, but it's not like a joint, it's—" Gabby makes a sound like an "oof," and the line goes dead.

Shit.

Shit shit shit.

So, not weed. Unfortunately, there's all sorts of nasty things that can be smoked. Crack. Heroin. Meth. All stuff even I avoid, and I'm far from responsible when it comes to what I put in my body.

I doubt Felix would recognize any of them; I'm not even sure *I* could tell all the differences.

And if he's upset enough to be doing this in the first place, he might not even care. Not what he takes, or how much, or with what other drugs . . .

That fear is blaring into an all-out panic.

What's the address? I text, even though I have no idea how I'll get there.

Shortly after, Gabby texts me back. I recognize the address—I hit up parties on that street a lot. I was at the frat house just down that street six months ago when a guy ODed. I didn't see it, just read about it the next day. I'd already left that morning before they found him, half-naked in the pantry, curled up around a box of Froot Loops.

Rumor was, he was a newbie user.

No, no, no. If Felix hurts himself, if Felix—I can't even think the words.

I have to get there, now.

I look around frantically for someone I can get a ride with. Someone—

My eyes land on Ian's car.

That'll do.

On my way, I text. Then I sprint back into the house. If I know Ian, he's already too high to drive, but that comes with another benefit—he'll also be too high to care if I borrow his car. I run from room to room, shoving people aside as necessary, ignoring their glares or slurred swears. Pierced eyebrow guy from before is already up on some other girl, and gives me a look like he hopes I'll change my mind and come join them, but I jog past them and into a bedroom in the back of the house.

And find Ian being straddled by a topless girl with long red hair, his face buried in her tits, as I had predicted.

"Ian!" I grab his shoulder and yank him back from her

enough to see me around her boobs.

"Hey!" the girl says, but she doesn't actually sound that upset about it; she's pretty stoned.

Ian scowls at me. "Whaaaat the hellll?" It's a long drawn-out sound. He's on something too, probably a mix of weed and pills.

"I need your keys."

He blinks; his eyes are big and dilated, and having trouble focusing on me. "My keys," he says.

"For your car." I'm having trouble not shaking him. "I. Need. Your. Car. Keys."

Ian makes a little groaning sound, but starts patting his pants pockets, so I think he might finally understand.

The red-haired girl yawns and then giggles, like she's amused by her own sleepiness. Or maybe her nipples, which she's rubbing absentmindedly. Oh my god, is this what I look like when I'm high or super drunk? I'm really glad Felix never saw me like this, or he'd—

He'd still love me, I think. He'd keep me safe. He'd make sure no one took advantage of me.

My heart squeezes so tight I'm afraid it'll burst.

If anything bad happens to him, it's my fault. I did this to him. And now I'm not there to make sure he's okay.

I know there's some faulty logic in there somewhere, but I'm too panicked to care.

Ian is struggling to get the keys out of his pants pockets, and I swear and reach in his pocket and grab it out myself, which prompts another giggle from the topless girl. Ian squints at me. "My car . . ." he says, uncertainly, turning back to the boobs in front of his face.

"Will be fine. I'll get it back to you . . . somehow." I don't have a plan for any of this, and thankfully, he's way too out of it to care.

I run back through the house, down the street, pushing through the pain of each step, and get into his car.

The drive is about twenty minutes, and it's nerve-wracking in more ways than one. Not having a car myself—and never taking the family car when I go out to a party, because what if there was an emergency in the night and Ty needed to go to the hospital or something?—I haven't actually driven anywhere since I got my license almost two years ago. This might not be an issue if I was willing to take my time, but going anywhere even close to the speed limit feels like I'm just inching along.

So I speed most of the way, narrowly miss crashing Ian's Neon into a median and then later a parked BMW, and I'm really, really grateful I didn't have any more to drink than that half beer.

And the whole way, I can't stop panicking about Felix.

Which is ridiculous, I try to tell myself. *You, Jenna Rollins, who go to parties and drink yourself to blacking-out and take pills and wake up with guys who could have done anything to you. You are worried about someone taking random drugs handed to them.*

People do stuff like this all the time, I tell myself. *And they're fine.*

Except they aren't always fine. Not even when they think they are.

And I know Felix. If he's doing this, he isn't fine. He isn't okay. And it's my fault.

I make it to fraternity row, and of course there's no parking. I swear some more. Then I double park on the street in front of the frat house and hope I'm not going to have to use my piano money to pay Ian back for his car getting towed.

There are people milling about in the lawn, and one guy yells at me to re-park, but I storm past him and into the house. The music is thumping so loud it makes my head buzz after every beat—a sensation I usually like, because it means the rest of me is about to get buzzed, too, and I can just lose myself in the music and the crowd. But now I have no desire to lose myself. I only want to find Felix.

I pass the guys at the keg, ignoring the cup of beer one of them thrusts at me with a "Hey, baby," and look through the kitchen, not seeing him or Gabby there. There are couples dancing all up on each other, but he's not one of them, or one of the couples with their hands all under each other's clothes in the living room, though I check anyway. Not that I think Gabby would have called me if she'd found Felix hooking up with some other girl, but it's possible he might have gotten with someone in the last half hour.

The thought hurts so much more than it has any right to.

I'm not his girlfriend anymore. I stand in the kitchen and grip a nearby counter, letting that sink in. Again.

And that's when, after all the panic and fears, it finally occurs to me to wonder what on earth I'm planning to actually *do* here. Drag him out of a party he wants to be at, like I have any right to have a say in his life? Tell him he can't drown his sorrows in booze and sex, like I haven't been doing that on the regular since I was fourteen? Smack a crack pipe out of his hand?

Okay, maybe that last one.

I don't know that I can do anything to help him, but I at least have to find him. I told Gabby I'd try.

And god, I just need to know he isn't doing something he can never come back from. I need to know I'm not going to read tomorrow morning about him ODing in a frat house.

And maybe, I just need to see him again.

I'm passing the stairs to the basement when my arm is grabbed, and I almost smack the person until I see it's Gabby.

"Jenna!" she says, and throws her arms around me. I'm too stunned to hug her back, and she doesn't seem to expect it. She pulls back, and I can see her brown eyes are wide. She's wearing a plain t-shirt and jeans, and has her blond hair back in a ponytail, and honestly, even in a total fade-into-the-background outfit like that, somehow couldn't stand out more in a scene like this.

"Where's Felix?" I ask—or yell, really.

She tugs me down the stairs into the basement. The music is slightly more muted here, the cheers from the wet t-shirt contest that had just started in the dining room slightly less obnoxious, but still too loud to speak naturally. She doesn't need to speak, anyway—she just points.

And there's Felix, slumped on a ratty couch, his head in his hands. My chest squeezes in so much at seeing him, I can't breathe again for a moment. Next to him, and sitting on the floor near him, are a bunch of what looks like college freshmen, drinking and laughing and passing around a vape mod.

I don't see a crack pipe or anything like that, but that doesn't mean they didn't have one.

"Felix!" I say, kneeling down by him. His head jerks up, blinking. He looks around wildly before he sees where I actually am.

"Jenna." His eyes go wide. Then he breathes out a laugh soaked in bitterness and beer. "You're not here. You're not really here. You left me. I'm high, so I'm just imagining you."

My heart cracks open. "I'm here, Felix." I grab his hand, which feels limp in mine. His speech is a little slurred, but his eyes don't look all crazy dilated or anything. "What did you take?"

"I wanted to go away," he says, closing his eyes.

"He's *so* wasted," a girl next to me says with a snicker, and I round on her, and the rest of him.

"What the *hell* did you guys give him? If you gave him meth or heroin or shit like that, so help me god, I will—"

"Whoa, chill," a guy with a patchy goatee and thick glasses says. "We didn't give him anything. Just this." He waggles the vape mod, and I snatch it out of his hand.

"Felix, is *this* what you smoked?" I turn to Gabby, who has walked up behind me. "Is this what he smoked?"

She nods, and I nearly collapse in relief. And also want to strangle her and Felix and every one of these hipster idiots sitting around me.

"Oh my god, Felix," I say, "Did you seriously go to a frat party and *vape*? You are so preppy." That last bit comes out as this relieved laugh.

Felix blinks at me blearily, then reaches for the mod. "You're not here, dream Jenna. I'm high."

"You vaped! You are not high!" I yell, then turn to Gabby and shove the vape box in her face. "Did you seriously think this was hard drugs? Oh my god."

She both gapes and winces, and I feel bad for yelling at her. Though really, who is this sheltered?

My boyfriend and his sister, apparently.

"I'm sorry, I—I just," she stammers. "This isn't like him, and he was so upset, and he said he wanted to get high, and—"

"Okay, yeah," I say. "This isn't like him. And he's definitely drunk."

"It doesn't feel better," Felix mumbles, slumping back. "It still hurts."

I put my arms around him and he leans into me, and god, it feels so good, even though he reeks like a few different kinds of alcohol and I know he's hurting, ripped apart inside, because of me.

I did this to him. I'd thought I did the right thing, letting him go so I wouldn't ruin his life.

But seeing him now, like this, so not-Felix, hurting so badly with a pain I know all too well, wanting to do anything to just disappear . . .

"Come on, Felix," I say quietly, right up against his ear. "Let's go back home, okay?"

"No," he says. "Not to them. They took you away. I hate them." Tears leak down his cheeks, and I feel my own eyes water.

I hug him tighter. "I'll come with you, okay?"

"You'll stay with me?"

I don't know how to answer that, not really. I want to, desperately. Forever. But Juilliard and his future and . . .

I look into his eyes, which are bloodshot and hopeful, and I give him a little smile.

"I'll be with you when you wake up," I say. "I promise."

That seems to be enough to get him on his feet, and between Gabby and I, we maneuver him through the house, propping him up as he staggers outside.

I put him in the Neon, where he promptly slumps into the passenger seat, almost asleep.

"Jenna, thanks so much," Gabby says, and I can see she's in tears herself. "I'm so sorry to drag you out here, especially if he wasn't really in trouble, but I just . . ."

I give her a hug, too, and she stiffens in surprise, but then hugs me back.

"It's okay," I say. "I'm sorry I yelled, I just was so scared, I—" I let out a breath. "I'm glad you called me."

She gives me a hesitant smile. "You really love him, don't you?"

"Yes," I say. There's no reason to lie to her. "I really do."

Her smile turns sad. "He loves you, too." She looks down at her feet. "My parents aren't always right, you know."

My gut twists, and I don't know what to say in response to that. "We'd better get him back. It's only a matter of time before he vomits all over my friend's car."

She nods and looks up again. "Thanks again, Jenna."

I grimace. "Don't thank me yet. I'll get him back to your house, but I promised I'd stay with him. Which means we need to drop this piece of shit masquerading as a vehicle back at the party I took it from, and then you need to drive us back to your house from there."

"No problem," she says. Then she hugs me again, and heads off to find their car, and I buckle in the driver's seat next to Felix.

"Jenna?" he murmurs, shifting but not really opening his eyes. "Are you still here?"

"I'm here, Felix," I say. "I'm not going anywhere."

TWENTY

Felix

I wake up to a pounding headache, and the worst-tasting morning breath I've ever had. I open my eyes, and the light in my dim room is too much. I squeeze them closed again.

And then my fingers brush against Jenna's arm under the covers.

I open my eyes again and she's there, still in her clothes from yesterday. I vaguely remember her showing up at the party last night, wreathed in light like an angel. I told her she wasn't real and she said she'd stay with me. It feels like I'm dreaming, but when I reach out and put a hand on her arm again, it feels real, and I don't remember ever having a headache this bad in a dream.

"Jenna," I say.

She opens her eyes. "Felix," she says softly.

"You broke up with me." I'm not so much accusing her as trying to discern what's real and what isn't. If she broke up with me, she shouldn't be here. She couldn't have been at that party—what are the odds we would have picked the same one?

"I did."

"Because of my mom."

Jenna's gray eyes are so deep, and filled with sadness. "Because

188

I think you deserve better than me, and I want you to be happy."

I shake my head, which only makes it ache more, and I wince.

She sits up and guides me to sit up too, even though I don't want to move. "I found some Advil in your medicine cabinet," she says, reaching across me to my nightstand, where I see a glass of water and a bottle of ibuprofen. "I figured you'd need that this morning."

I twist off the cap and swallow a couple of the pain meds with some water. The pills are bitter, but miles better than how the inside of my mouth tasted before.

I'm grateful, but I know that what I really need is her. And she's here now, but I don't know how long that will be true.

I set the glass back on the nightstand and look over at her, sitting up against the headboard beside me. She's close enough to me that our shoulders brush. "You said you want me to be happy," I say. "But I was happy with you."

Jenna's gaze drops. "But you'd always planned to go to Juilliard, and I've made you doubt what you wanted. You can't give away a dream like that for me."

I bite my lip. Jenna seems hesitant about all this. I hate what she's saying, but she doesn't seem as certain about it as she did before. "My parents planned on me going to Juilliard. I first picked up the cello when I was ten years old, and by eleven, my parents had my future all planned out. And yeah, I wanted it. I worked for it. I like playing, and I like being the best, and if you play and you're the best you're supposed to want Juilliard. I thought, once I got there, maybe I'd get to be happy."

"That's what your mom says." Her voice shakes slightly. "That you'd be so happy when you got there."

"But then I met you," I say. "And suddenly I *was* happy. Because I thought you loved me. Because I thought I'd finally found someone who saw more than just the music. But that's all it was, wasn't it? You heard me play, and you connected to that, and you wanted to be with me for a minute, but then I'm expected to just go to New York all by myself and become a better musician. Other people get to choose what they want based on how they feel, but I have to be a robot who plays, and I have to be the best, and if I'm not, no one will give a shit about me."

Jenna's eyes shine with tears, and she pulls herself closer to me. "No," she says. "I love your music, and I think it's so sexy how much you love it. And I selfishly want you to give up all those things you dreamed about and be with me, but not because of the music. Because I love *you*. And if you never played again in your life, that would still be true."

I shiver. I want to believe that. I want it to be true so badly it hurts.

"But," Jenna says, and that word cuts through me like a knife. "I want you to be happy. And I'm not sure how I could ever be enough. I know you want me now, but the idea that you'd give up something so important and then someday regret it—"

"Do I get a say in what I want?"

Jenna looks up at me. A tear slips down her cheek, but she holds my gaze. "What do you want?"

I'm afraid to tell her. I'm so afraid to open my heart to her again, afraid that in the end, she's not going to want me back, not the way I want her.

"I want to be a family," I say. "Me and you, and Ty." She flinches, and I pull her closer. We settle back into the bed, so we're lying beside each other, both of our heads on my pillow. "Not today, but someday. I want to work toward that, so that someday the three of us can live together in some little apartment. And I might want to go to music school, but I think first I'd like to see if I could get work playing. There are a lot more orchestra jobs than there are spots at Juilliard, and I'm good, and I can work my ass off to get better. I could audition everywhere that will let me in LA, and see if I could find something. And if not, then I could always go to music school somewhere around here."

I take a deep breath. I'm not sure my parents would pay for anywhere but Juilliard. I'm not sure they're going to be speaking to me if I go through with any of this. But I'd figure it out somehow. I might be able to get a scholarship, even. "But if I could break in, I could get paid to play, instead of paying for it. And I could support us. And then you could stay home with Ty, if you wanted. Or we could both work and juggle him around, and I'm sure your parents would still watch him, but maybe your mom could go back to work if she wanted, or—"

"You really want all that," Jenna says.

"Yeah," I say. "Do you?"

"I still don't know if I can be a mom to Ty," she says quietly. "Would you still want to be with me if I couldn't?"

I can't imagine *not* wanting to be with her, ever. "Of course I do. Then you and I would be a family. But I want you to be happy, and it seems like you really want to try with him."

"I do, actually. I mean, I'm still scared I'll mess it up. But I'd like to try. I think maybe I'm ready for that much, at least." She looks down at our interlocked fingers, and then squeezes her eyes shut. "I know this doesn't make sense, since I'm the one who had ended things, but I'm just—I'm so scared to lose you."

I shake my head. "You're not going to lose me. Not unless you decide to walk away."

Jenna starts crying, and buries her face in my chest. I hold her close as sobs wrack her body, and I wish I could take away whatever's hurting her so bad.

"I don't know how any of you could be happy with me," she sobs. "With the things I've done, the person I am. I'm not someone you should want."

I stroke her hair, gently. "I want you," I tell her. "What happened to you—it's not you. It's not who you are."

"But I chose it," Jenna says. "I kept going back for more, even though I knew what would happen. Even though I knew I wouldn't even remember everything that had happened. I don't know why I did that. I really don't. But I must be a really awful person to want that."

"Do you want it now?" I ask.

Jenna sniffles against my shirt. "No. I went to a party last night, but I didn't do anything. This guy hit on me, and I didn't want any part of it, and so I yelled at him and I left, and then I got a call from Gabby—"

Ah. So that's how she got there. "Gabby called you?"

"Yeah," she says. "To tell me you were getting high and I needed to help you get out of there."

I vaguely remember smoking something out of this metal, box-like pipe, and then Jenna yelling at me about— "I was vaping."

"Yes," she says, looking up at me. Her face is tear-stained, but she's smiling. "You were not high. You were vaping. Neither of you seemed to know the difference."

I laugh with her. "I definitely did not."

"And I was glad," Jenna says. "Because hypocritical as it was, I was so scared you were going to OD, or get hooked on something, and I couldn't stand the idea of you getting hurt because of what I did to you."

"No. What I did last night wasn't your fault."

"It was," she says. "Because I let you get near me, and I hurt people."

"Who? Who do you hurt?"

Jenna sniffles again. "My parents."

"Your parents love you. I've met them twice and I know that."

"Rachel. Ty."

"Who also love you. I mean, yeah, you and Rachel don't get along, right? You should see me and Gabby with our older sister Dana. That's normal, Jenna."

Jenna shakes her head. "No. She just wants me to not be an idiot and throw my life away. She just wants me to be a mother to my kid. It's not her fault we don't get along."

"Okay," I say. "But it's normal not to get along with your siblings. And it's probably really normal to be a teen mother who has a fraught relationship with the kid she loves so much but isn't ready to be a mother to. You think you're a horrible person, but it all seems really understandable to me."

"Maybe. But I've been hurting and worrying them all for years, and now I've done it to you."

I nod against her hair. "And are you going to go out to parties and cheat on me and break my heart?"

"No," Jenna says. "No, I wouldn't cheat on you, ever. And the parties—I think I'm done with parties. That one last night—I didn't want to be there. I just wanted to be with you."

I smile. I could stand to hear that about a thousand times more. "You're safe now," I say. "And so am I. I have someone who wants things from me that aren't just about music. Someone I matter to as a person, for who I am. Someone I can build a future with. You make me feel like I matter to you, just for being me, and I need that more than anything in the world. A hell of a lot more than Juilliard."

Jenna starts crying again, but she's clinging to me tight. "And I need you. Because you make me feel loved and safe and worth something."

"You are worth something," I say. "You're worth *everything* to me. I'm just sorry I took so long to find you."

Jenna giggles through her tears. "You're seventeen. You could have taken a lot longer."

I laugh. "Yeah, I suppose I could have."

We hold each other, and even though my head is still dully aching, just being with her like this again, hearing that she still wants this, wants me—it's incredible. And though I'm pretty sure we're officially back together, I still have to ask. "So are we back on for prom?"

"Yes," Jenna says. "If you still want to take me."

"Of course I do. And I meant what I said before. If you want to save your money for a piano, you don't need to buy a dress." Though I'm realizing now that if my parents cut me off financially—which they are likely to when they discover I'm

193

back with Jenna and not backing down about Juilliard—I have enough to buy prom tickets, but there won't be much left over.

Jenna must sense what I'm thinking, or else her mind is following the same trail as mine. It's Saturday morning. My parents are home, and I'd give it even odds they know Jenna's here.

"What about your parents?" she asks.

"They might disown me."

"For dating me?"

"For refusing to apply to Juilliard. For dating you. For generally insisting I be allowed to make my own decisions." Oh, god. It could get a lot worse than just cutting off my allowance. "It's possible I won't be able to stay here. Not that I think they're likely to throw me out on the street, but it could easily get bad enough that living here would be untenable."

She chews at her lower lip. "If that happened—I think my parents would let you stay with us."

"Really?" I say. Her parents are nice—to me, anyway—but I have a hard time seeing them thinking it's a great idea for their daughter to shack up with her underage boyfriend under their roof.

"Yeah," Jenna says. "They like you, and since we're going to be together, they'll want to make sure you can finish school, and that we're both safe. They won't be crazy about us having sex, but compared to what they've had to deal with me doing over the last several years—"

I smile. "Maybe we shouldn't tell them about last night. That would probably make me less attractive to them."

"Yes. Because vaping isn't attractive to anyone."

I tickle her waist, and she shrieks and laughs and slaps my arm.

"Okay," I say. "I deserved that. And I'm never going to live that down."

"You are not, and neither is your sister."

"I bet Gabby's really embarrassed about that, but I'm so glad she called you."

Jenna softens against me. "Me too."

"You know, next year, it's possible we could make it so your mom could go back to work," I say. "That might help make up for them having another mouth to feed, if I can't stay here."

Jenna considers this. "I'll need to get a job, so I'd probably be gone during the day. I guess I could get a night job, but then I'd never see you, and—"

"What if we both taught lessons?" I ask. "I've never been excited about teaching cello to kids who don't want to practice, but I could, if it was something I was doing to build our future. And lessons are mostly after school anyway, because that's when kids are available. And I could finish school independent study, and help you take care of Ty, and then we could work in the afternoon when your mom is home, and then in the evening, we could have time to ourselves. When I'm not doing homework, I guess—"

"Yes," Jenna says. "Because I've been so good about letting you do homework."

I laugh. "I'll have to do some sometime. I do want to keep my grades up so I can get into music school in a couple years, if I need to."

"You really want this. Even though you think your parents are going to make your life so miserable that you'll have to leave," Jenna says, still looking at me like she can't quite believe it, like it might be too good to be true. And having her here with me again after I thought I'd lost her forever—I get that feeling.

"Yes," I say. "More than I've ever wanted anything in my life." And it's true. I know we're young, and I know that future involves a lot of responsibility, a lot of work, and that's not going to be easy. But I've never had a problem working hard towards a goal—and I can't imagine a goal more worthy than this.

"I still feel like I'm taking something away from you."

I shake my head and hold her tight. "You're not. You're giving me so many things that they're hard to count. My life feels so bright and full with you in it." I look down at her, run my thumb along her jaw. "I love you, Jenna. And I want us to keep loving each other for the rest of our lives."

"I don't know how I could ever stop," she says. And then she scoots up and kisses me.

And if it's a dream, I hope I never wake up.

TWENTY-ONE

Jenna

It's the Tuesday before prom, and instead of spending my afternoon with Felix having yet another round of incredible make-up sex—which we've determined we can call it for at least a solid week, given how traumatic the break-up was for both of us—I am dress shopping at a thrift store. With my mom. And my sister.

Shockingly, I am not miserable about this.

"How about this one?" my mom asks, holding up a long sleek slip dress in robin's egg blue.

Rachel and I wrinkle our noses simultaneously.

"What?" My mom frowns. "I think it's elegant."

"I'm sure it was," I say. "In 1997. When Gwyneth Paltrow or one of the chicks from *Friends* wore it to the Teen Choice Awards."

Rachel snorts a little laugh, and Mom looks confused. "Is that a bad thing? Who wouldn't want to look like Gwyneth? Or Jennifer Aniston?"

"Me," I say pointedly. "Plus, it's really . . . blue."

Rachel rolls her eyes. "Yeah, god forbid you wear something not black."

"I wear other colors. Red. Gray. Various *shades* of black."

"Right. You're a veritable Crayola box of colors. The 'Emo' collection."

"You really want to get into a debate about fashion while wearing those wide-leg jeans?"

Rachel opens her mouth to say something back, but Mom cuts in. "Girls, come on." But her scolding is lacking the usual weary quality. Maybe because she can tell, too, that something is different about our bickering.

Rachel and I exchange small smiles.

We're teasing now, not fighting, and we both know it. I don't know that it will always be this way—who am I kidding, it probably won't be even through the rest of this week. But I think of the way Rachel was there for me when I was at my lowest, and I hope someday I can return the favor. And maybe along the way, I can be a better sister, and a better friend.

Baby steps.

"There's this lovely number," Rachel says, pulling what was obviously someone's awful bridesmaid dress off a rack. "It's red."

It is at that. A cherry red with a flouncy knee-length skirt with layers of tulle, and sweetheart neckline with big sleeves puffy enough to be used as flotation devices.

I laugh, and my mom makes a little hmmm-ing sound. "Maybe we should go to a real dress store," she says. "At the mall, maybe." But I can see her crunching the numbers in her head, trying to think of what else she can sell or go without to get me the perfect prom dress, and my heart cracks a little.

"No, Mom," I say. "It's just a dress. It's not worth that kind of money. Felix said I'd be fine wearing something I already have, even."

She gives me a sad smile. "But it's your prom, and you're going with a boy you love. It's important, and I want you to have the perfect dress."

Her eyes are getting a little shiny, and it feels like there's so much more behind those words, things she can't yet say. We've both been like that the last few days. Talking without really talking.

But it's better than not talking at all.

I reach out and squeeze her hand, a gesture that surprises us both. "I think I'll be able to find the perfect dress here," I say. "I find the best clothes at thrift stores. You just have to be willing to dig through a bunch of shit."

Mom's smile turns less sad, but her eyes still shine, and she squeezes my hand back so tightly I'm a little worried I'll get permanent nerve damage. But I don't pull away.

"Right. Like this beauty." Rachel shakes a day-glo orange dress with layers of fringe.

"Oooh." I grab it from her and hold it up to myself. "What do you think, Mom? Pair this with some go-go boots and I could go pole dancing and hunting all in the same day."

Now Rachel laughs outright, which makes me more than a little proud.

Mom throws her hands up in the air. "You girls are going to be the death of me," she says, but she's grinning.

We poke through the thrift store's offerings a while longer, laughing at the truly heinous fashion mistakes of days past, and eventually even I'm starting to lose faith in my thrifting abilities being good enough for prom. I'm frowning at a floral-patterned Southern Belle-type dress, wondering if anyone in the world—including Scarlett O'Hara herself—could have worn this non-ironically, when Mom speaks up next to me.

"Ty couldn't stop talking about how much fun he had at the park with you and Felix yesterday." She says this so casually, but she's a little too intensely staring at the sequins of someone's old dance costume for it to not be another one of those things that has so much weight behind it.

My chest squeezes in, even as I feel a little flutter of happiness. We did have fun yesterday, and I didn't lose him, which is an improvement over last time. There was a little meltdown when he spilled his raisins on the ground, but we all survived. "Really?"

"Yep. I bet he's still gabbing all about 'Super Ty' to Mrs. Wu and driving her crazy."

Mrs. Wu is our elderly next-door neighbor, who I have learned often watches Ty when Mom needs to run out for something, and is currently doing so for this dress-shopping expedition until my Dad gets home from work. I smile. "Isn't she hard of hearing? So maybe that's working in her favor today."

Mom chuckles. "Probably."

There's a beat of silence, and I find myself holding my breath, wondering if I should actually tell her about my and Felix's plans. For me to really be Ty's mom someday. For us to be a family.

I told her about the breakup, of course, and Juilliard, and his parent's reaction. And then about us getting back together, and how he's planning on staying here and trying to find work after he graduates next year, and how I could too, even if it's just teaching piano lessons. But doing all this together.

To say my parents were surprised would be an understatement. To say they were barely hiding their elation at me planning something so solid for my future—this plan being solid compared to the total lack of plan other than partying I had previous—would be even more of an understatement.

But I didn't mention how both Felix and I want Ty to fit into all this, and they didn't ask, other than to find out whether we were planning on living around here.

The thought of Felix and Ty and I being a real family, the three of us living in some apartment and us being his parents—I want it so badly and yet am still afraid I can't live up to it. Even though Felix said that if I couldn't, he'd still want to be with me, that he'd still want him and I together, always. Which I would too, of course. No matter what.

But I want *this* dream the most of all, and it scares me to say it out loud to anyone but him.

Yesterday at the park was great, but it didn't make that fear go away. I'm glad right now that Rachel's standing too far away from us to hear even this much—and that she seems to be too distracted in trying not to stare at the cute guy working the cash register.

"You know," my mom says, still in that too-casual tone. "He also really likes going to Storytime at the library on Thursday mornings. Once you're out of school, I'm sure he'd be thrilled if you wanted to come with us. Or even if you wanted to just take him yourself, or with Felix."

Storytime at the library, with my son. Not something I ever saw myself doing.

But I'm at a thrift store looking for a dress for prom with the guy I'm in love with, and am planning a future with, so apparently lots of things are changing.

And this, like the rest of it, sounds like a really good change. If still a bit terrifying.

"Yeah," I say, toying with the floppy bow on the Southern Belle dress's waist. "That could be cool."

Mom gives me a little smile that confirms she's already figured out my plans regarding Ty, or at least my hopes. I'm partially relieved I don't have to say it, and partially even more nervous—it feels like just one more person to potentially let down.

But maybe it's okay if I do. I mean, I've done that plenty already, but we're still here now, dress shopping.

A family.

Which reminds me. "Hey, Mom," I say, and she looks up from a row of scarves.

"Yes?"

"You know how I told you about how crazy Felix's parents are about him going to Juilliard?"

Her lips press together tightly. She really didn't like hearing about the things Felix's mom said to me—or to him, for that matter. "Crazy sounds like the operative word there."

"Right." I shift back and forth. "Well, they still haven't con-fronted him about us getting back together, or the fact that he

201

said he isn't going. But they will, someday. And . . . we don't know how that's going to go, but Felix's guess is not well. Like *really* not well."

"Okay," she says cautiously.

"There's a chance they might threaten to kick him out of their house. Or at least make it so miserable for him there that he'll need to get out."

Her eyebrows raise to her hairline. "They would actually do that? His parents?" And I kind of get where the shock comes from. My parents have had a daughter who got pregnant at fourteen, did drugs and partied and pretty much made them crazy with worry non-stop since, and they have never threatened something like that.

I think back to Felix telling me that his parents don't really care about him, but I don't think that's true. I talked to his mom, and I could see that she cares. But I don't think they know how to separate caring for him from caring for what they think is best for him—and it makes me sad that I got caught in that trap as well for a little bit.

At least on my end, it had nothing to do with what I could brag about to my brunch friends. Ugh.

"They might," I say. "I told him if that happened, you guys would probably be okay if he moved in with us." I chew on the inside of my lip. "Is that true?"

Mom considers, and I find myself holding my breath. Finally, she speaks again. "We love Felix already, and love how happy he makes you," she says. "And how he is with Ty. Even your dad agrees on that. So, yeah. I'm sure we would be happy to have him stay with us, as long as he needed to."

I smile, the tightness in my chest loosening.

Then my mom says, "Though we don't have an extra bedroom, so he might have to sleep in the den."

I groan. "Oh my god, Mom, he is not sleeping in the—" I cut off, seeing how she's fighting to hide a laugh. "You're just messing with me, aren't you?"

"Yes I am. I'm perfectly aware he would move into your bedroom."

"What?" Rachel's voice sounds behind me, and I cringe. "Is Felix *moving in* now?"

I look back at her. "Not anytime soon, but maybe someday." I both want to ask *is that okay*, and don't. Because I'm not sure I want to hear the answer.

"Huh." Rachel says, like she's taking it in, and then shakes her head. "This family gets weirder and weirder." But she gives me a half-smile. "It's cool, though. I'm over it."

I give her a smile back. I don't know if that's totally true, but I believe it will be. She never really knew Felix, and from the way her gaze keeps cutting away to the guy in the register, I have a feeling Felix will have been far from the only guy she's into this year.

"You know, you could go actually *talk* to him instead of just creepily staring at him over my shoulder," I say, looking back at register-guy, and she flushes.

"I know how to talk to boys!" she grouses.

"Do you? Because—"

"Girls," Mom warns again. "We're here on a mission, remember? And that mission is not to get Rachel a boyfriend with a lip ring."

Now my eyebrows are raised, and I swivel to look back at the register guy. "He has a lip ring?" I give her approving nod. "Damn, Rachel. Just watch out for that when you guys—"

"Jenna!" Mom's got her hands up over her face.

Rachel and I both bust up laughing.

"Okay, fine. We're here for a dress." I sigh and look around, as if the perfect prom dress will magically appear from the racks we've already been through. And then my gaze lands on that red bridesmaid number Rachel picked out earlier—or at the least the flouncy skirt part that's jutting out past the other clothes. The skirt part that might actually be kind of cute, if it wasn't attached to the Valentine's Wedding Nightmare of the top half.

And I have an idea.

"Mom," I say, slowly. "Remember when you used to find clothes at places like this and alter them to make Halloween costumes for us?"

"Oh yes. And I would hear all about how unfair it was that you girls had to wear hand-made costumes instead of store bought ones."

Rachel snorts. "Only because I had to be Raggedy Ann two years in a row."

I brush aside the fact that at least she didn't have to be Raggedy *Andy*, which was the real trial.

"How do you feel about busting out the sewing machine again?" I ask, pulling the dress off the rack, and waving it around a little. Rachel looks at me like I'm crazy, but my mom's eyes brighten, and I think she gets where I'm going with this.

I don't think we're going to find the perfect dress. I think we're just going to have to make it.

We get back home and Felix joins us all for dinner, which my dad has ready for us. Sure, it's grilled cheese sandwiches and Snapple, but we all appreciate the effort. After dinner, we play with Ty until Mom announces it's his bedtime—man, three-year-olds have early bedtimes. Then Felix and I go out for a bit, to spend some time just the two of us.

He has an idea, he says. Then he gets us Frosties at the Wendy's drive-through and we drive up to that dirt lot where you can see the Hollywood sign. And I sit in his lap, and we hold each other and talk and talk, and it's all just so incredible and right.

We do lots of other things, too, of course, which also feel pretty damn incredible and right.

It's hard to believe how very, very different my life is—how different I feel, and how happy—from when we drove here last time, just over a week ago. It's hard to believe the place we're at now, Felix and me. Talking about our future, together.

Then again, I remember the way he made me feel even then, how he's always made me feel, and maybe it's not so hard to believe, after all.

Hours later, Felix drops me back home, and I'm making my way to my room, feeling so good it's like I'm floating.

And then I hear a soft crying sound coming from Ty's room.

I pause in front of the partially-open door. He's definitely crying, though not in the tantrum way he did at the park with the spilled raisins. It's this sad little hopeless sound, and it breaks my heart.

Maybe my mom's already in there, helping him. Or maybe I should get her—she's way more likely to know how to help him than I am. I peek my head in, but she's not there.

There's some more little sniffles, and then Ty's voice. "Mommy?"

My nerves flare, but I step inside anyway, and sit down on the edge of his bed. "What's wrong, Ty?"

"I can't find mist m-muff," he says, his voice trembling. "I need seep wif him."

"Mister Muffles?" That's right, that was the name of that woolly mammoth toy I put back in his bed last week. He *does* still sleep with him! I feel a surge of triumph, at least until I see Ty's tear-streaked face. "Okay, let's see if we can find him," I say. "He can't have wandered off too far." The light of the nightlight doesn't extend much past the head of the bed, so I crawl around investigating every dark lump on Ty's floor that looks vaguely Mister Muffles-sized. I end up with a pile of clothes, and what I think is a stuffed monkey, but no woolly mammoth.

"Hmmm," I say, talking quietly as I go. "Mister Muffles, are you next to the dresser? Nope, not there. Are you in the closet? Doesn't look like it. Are you . . . on the ceiling? Nope, that's the fan."

That last one makes Ty giggle, and the sound warms my heart. Even as I'm starting to worry I may not be able to find the missing mammoth.

And then I notice a lump under his bed, and my hand closes around that familiar woolly fur. "A-ha, there you are, Mister Muffles!" I swing him back up onto the bed, and Ty throws his arms around him and hugs him tight. "I think he likes tight spaces as much as you do, buddy."

Ty snuggles back up on his pillow, a smile on his face, even as the nightlight still glistens on the tear tracks running down his cheeks. "You okay now?" I ask, hesitant. Do I leave now? Do I stay?

He nods, but his eyes are wide open, watching me, and I remember that Dad used to sing a song to him before he went to sleep. Does he still do that?

"Do you want me to sing something to you?"

Ty nods again.

I'm about to ask what song he likes, when I remember a song my dad used to sing to me, a long, long time ago, when I used to wake up with nightmares and try to crawl into bed with them.

"Okay," I say, and stroke his soft blond hair. And then I start singing "Danny's Song." It's been ages, but I remember every word. Ty's eyes close, and his hand grips onto my fingers, and I find myself choking up, stumbling over the lyrics, "I'm so in love with you, honey."

Because it's true, I am. He's my son. And as I sing softly, until his breathing gets even and deep, I feel for the first time that being his mom isn't just something I hope I can do someday, but that it really is something I can do. Something I will. I finish the song, but I sit there awhile, watching my son sleep. Feeling his little hand clinging to mine.

And finally, finally, I feel that's true. It's not going to be easy, necessarily, but everything is going to be all right.

TWENTY-TWO

Felix

To save money for prom, I wear a suit I already had. My parents didn't say anything about cutting off my allowance, but they also didn't make a deposit in my account this week. I assume they're waiting for me to come beg for it, and that's not going to happen.

Gabby suggests I can grab some flowers at the craft store and make a wrist corsage that won't go bad for half the price, which turns into a grand misadventure in which Gabby and I repeatedly wrap our fingers together with floral tape, while the sprigs with rose blossoms on them flop uselessly off of the elastic band. The YouTube video makes it look so easy, but Gabby is picking floral tape off her index finger for the dozenth time when my mother walks in on this disaster spread over the kitchen table, and Gabby and I both fall silent.

My mother walks over, looking at the damage. She raises an eyebrow at Gabby. "I thought we had given up on your passion for flower arranging," she says dryly.

Gabby's cheeks turn pink, and I shake my head. "It's mine, actually. I was trying to make a corsage for Jenna."

My mom purses her lips, and I expect her to make some nasty comment about a cheap corsage for a cheap girl, but instead she picks up the elastic band and the floral tape, and wraps the stems of the red roses with a few quick loops. She picks up a few sprigs of leaves that have fallen by the wayside and pushes them through the tape, securing them in place. And then she hands the results to me. I put them on my wrist, to test them.

The corsage is perfect.

"Thanks, Mom," I say.

She looks at me for a long moment. I can't tell if she's regretting helping me, or just regretting that her son has wandered so far astray.

"Jenna's parents will take pictures," she says.

I'm surprised that she cares. "Yes," I tell her.

She nods. "Good." And then strides out of the kitchen without another word.

Gabby looks at me wide-eyed, and I shrug. I know another confrontation is coming. I know I haven't heard the end of Juilliard, and I'm going to have to figure out how to pay for my car insurance and gas and so forth, so I'll probably be teaching lessons even if I am still staying here for a while, and looking for real work on the side.

But the truth is, there isn't anything my parents can do to stop me from working toward a future with Jenna. If they try, I'll walk out. My parents are far too concerned with image to report me as a runaway. I'm pretty sure they're hoping the lack of money will get me to shape up, but they're wrong.

I'll walk this tightrope with them as long as I can, because they're my parents, and I don't want to be the reason they're not in my life. But if they cut the rope out from under me, I have a net to catch me.

Thanks to Jenna, I don't have far to fall.

When I arrive at Jenna's place to pick her up, Ty comes to the door with Jenna's mom. He's wearing a satin cape and a little suit complete with vest. "Look!" he shouts at me. "I'm a genelmem."

"Gentleman," Mrs. Rollins translates.

"You sure are, kid," I say, kneeling down.

"I think Jenna's still getting ready," Mrs. Rollins says. "But Felix, you look like quite the gentleman yourself."

I smile, and speak conspiratorially to Ty. "Hey, can you help me with something?" I pull out the corsage. "Can you give this to your mom?"

"Ooooh," Ty says. "Fowers."

I smile. "Yep, flowers. It's for your mom to wear on her wrist." I slide it on to his, hoping he's not about to pick all the petals off before Jenna even sees it. "Like this."

Ty gets this big beaming smile. "I give it her," he says, and then he turns and runs up the stairs shouting "Mooooooooom!"

I smile. It's a little terrifying, thinking of being responsible for his well-being someday. I feel like I'm barely ready to be responsible for my own. But Mrs. Rollins invites me in to sit on the couch, and I look at the family pictures on the wall. There are several of Jenna when she was little, when her hair was brown instead of dyed black. But all the ones over the last few years have Ty in them. Smiling with Rachel, riding on his grandfather's shoulders. Even one in Jenna's arms at the hospital when he was born.

Ty already has a family. If Jenna and I can't take care of him, he's already in good hands. In fact, standing here in their home, I can't help but feel like an interloper. My family is so different from Jenna's. I can't imagine how I could ever fit in.

"Are you admiring my bangs?" Jenna asks. I turn around, and she's pointing to a picture of her and Rachel, in which she has classic four-year-old fringe, the kind that begin on the crown of her head.

I want to say something witty back, but instead I stare at her.

209

She's wearing a red skirt with layers of voluminous underskirt that sticks out above her knees, with one of her black lace-up corsets. Her hair is down over one shoulder, and swept up on the other side and pinned back with a silver barrette. Her black boots almost reach her knees, and the corsage of red roses is already on her wrist. She toys with the band.

"Thanks," she says.

I smile. "You look amazing."

She grins at me. "So do you."

"Pictures!" Jenna's mom says from behind her, and I grab Jenna's hand, and then she's in my arms. We turn around and smile for the camera, while Ty runs in circles around us with his hands and cape both flying out behind him.

"Ty!" Jenna's mom says. "Come stand by me and help me take the picture."

"Eh," Jenna says. "He's already dressed like a gentleman. Come here, Ty."

She scoops him up and rests him on her hip like he belongs there, and all three of us smile for the camera.

When Jenna's mom is done snapping pictures—mostly because Jenna told her to be finished already or we're going to be late—I ask her to text me a few, so that I can show my mom. She texts several at both of us, and on the way to dinner, I catch Jenna fiddling with her phone.

"Looking at those pictures?" I ask.

"Saving them," she says, but there's something guilty about her expression.

"What?"

She gives me a sideways look and holds up her phone. She's set one of the ones of us with Ty as her background.

A lump forms in my throat. It takes me a moment to figure out why.

It's possible that's our very first family photo, the kind that might be on a wall like the one at Jenna's house, covered in images from over the years. I reach over and take Jenna's hand.

I want to do everything I can not to mess that up.

P rom is being held in the ballroom of a hotel, and by the time we get there, the room is already full of people dancing. The ceiling is covered with a huge net containing little pieces of metallic confetti, which are filtering down through the air from the vibrations of the speakers set up on the other side of the room. The lights are dark and the music is hard to hear over the steady beat of the bass, at least for those of us not already on the dance floor. I see Daniel dancing with his date—it surprises me he has one, but on closer inspection, I'm pretty sure she's one of the girls who eats with him at the Mormon lunch table. They're dancing with their elbows locked so straight that you could fit two other people between them, but still. He's touching a girl. For Daniel, that's progress.

More people are standing around the walls of the room in groups, or clustered around tables drinking punch or looking over each other's shoulders to watch videos on their phones.

"So," Jenna says. "This is the elusive high school dance."

"In the flesh. Does it match your expectations?"

"I don't know. Want to stage some dramatic breakup on the dance floor? Where I scream at you for texting your ex and you yell at me for flirting with the gym teacher?"

I pull her close. "Tempting as that is," I say in her ear. "I never want to break up with you again."

Jenna looks up at me, and then we're kissing, and I can't hear anything except my heartbeat in my ears, aligning to the beat from the enormous speakers behind the dance floor.

"Felix!" someone yells, and I turn around to see my usual lunch table group standing right behind us. Julia is plastered up against the side of Chip Devlin, who I wasn't aware she was dating, although maybe he's just her date for prom. Angela's date is Spencer Cox, who has been trying to beat me out for first chair cello since fifth grade and failing. I think he gave up sometime last year, when I became the only junior to get first chair, pissing off all the seniors. He likes to pretend to be my friend, but I know he talks trash behind my back. He's kind of hilariously bad at concealing it.

"Hey," I say.

"Nice dress," Julia says to Jenna, with a kind of sour tone that clearly says she doesn't think it's a dress at all, let alone a nice one.

Jenna doesn't even blink. "Thank you!" she says, as if she thinks Julia is honestly complimenting her. "It's retro vintage chic. So in this year."

Julia looks stunned, and I smother a laugh. I'm pretty sure Jenna doesn't give a crap about what's in this year. Julia looks like she's formulating a comeback when Chip detaches himself from Julia and puts a hand on my shoulder. "So, how much for an hour with your date?" he asks.

It takes me a second for it to sink in what he's asking. "Excuse me?" I say.

"How much?" Chip says.

Julia is staring at Chip like she can't believe this is happening, and I feel kind of bad for her. I was a shitty boyfriend, but at least I never tried to solicit sex from someone else's date while we were together.

I let go of Jenna and turn, positioning myself between her and Chip. "What exactly are you saying about my girlfriend?"

"Come on," Chip says. "Everyone knows you're paying her."

I stare at Chip, and that's when I realize what people think. I negotiated the deal with Jenna in the middle of the lunchroom; I've been openly paying her after class. Of course the story has spun beyond the truth.

Of course people have decided that's what I'm doing with her.

Jenna grabs my arm. "It's okay, Felix."

But it isn't. It isn't okay for people to be saying that about her. "I paid her to do our homework," I say. "That's it."

Julia is trying to pull Chip away, but he brushes her off and laughs. "Sure, well I could use someone to do my homework, you know what I'm saying?"

I ball my fists. I've never hit anyone in my life, but I'm about

212

to get into a fight and cause that drama Jenna wanted right here and now. Chip has always been kind of a dick, but this is way too far, even for him.

Then, over the sound system, I hear the DJ asking how everybody's doing tonight, and I take a step back.

Jenna's right. He's not worth it. Besides, if I get into a fight with Chip over Jenna, people will just twist that to be part of the narrative.

I need to put an end to this story, once and for all.

"Go to hell, Chip," I say, and I turn and walk as fast as I can toward the table between the speakers where the DJ has his equipment set up. The next song begins, but I step over the thick bunches of cables running to the wall outlets and grab the DJ's microphone, and then stand up on the table, looking out over the room.

"What the fuck, man!" the DJ yells, but I ignore him.

"Hey," I yell into the microphone, and the DJ cuts the song, and people who were starting to grind all up on each other again on the dance floor spin around to stare at me.

I have their attention.

"I just heard," I say, "that there's a rumor going around about me and Jenna Rollins."

People start whispering to each other, and I see several smirks. It takes me a second to find Jenna. She's standing on the far side of the dance floor, looking at me like she has no idea what I'm doing.

"I just wanted to make it clear," I say, "that I'm in love with Jenna Rollins." I smile at her. "I love you, Jenna."

Jenna shakes her head at me like I'm a crazy person, but she's grinning. There's a stunned silence from the room, and I can see Mr. Simpson, the assistant principal, making his way around the dance floor toward me.

"Jenna is my girlfriend, and yeah, I paid her to do her half of our health project, because I didn't want to fail, but I'm dating her because I'm in love with her, and she's the most amazing person I've ever known, and I want to be with her for the rest of my life. Just wanted to clear that up."

I can hear Mr. Simpson yelling my name, and I drop back down to the floor and hand the microphone to the DJ. I hold my hands up in surrender, and Mr. Simpson seems to see that I'm stepping away now, and not causing any more trouble, because he lets me go with just a long glare, which he's clearly got down to a science.

I turn around and head back to Jenna, who meets me halfway across the floor.

"You didn't have to do that," she says.

I wrap my arms around her and pull her into me. "Yes, I did."

Jenna rests her head on my shoulder, and across the room, I spot Chip and Julia. "Hey," I say to Jenna as the music starts up again, fast and loud. "Check it out."

Jenna turns, and we watch as Julia throws her corsage right in Chip's face and tries to storm off. He grabs her by the hand, and she wrenches away, her face turning bright red. I can't hear what she's screaming at him over the music, but I have a pretty good idea.

"Oh, good," Jenna says. "There's the requisite dramatic break-up. My high school dance experience is complete."

"Not quite," I say. "We haven't danced yet." Jenna spins around, our arms slipping around each other's waists as we step onto the floor. People move aside, probably staying away because they don't know what to make of us.

And as we start to dance to the beat of the music, our bodies pressed up together, I don't care at all what they think. Because I'm with Jenna. I'm half of us. I'm crazy in love with the girl of my dreams, and I never, ever want it to stop.

ACKNOWLEDGMENTS

There are so many people we'd like to thank for helping make this book a reality. First, our families, especially our incredibly supportive husbands Glen and Drew, and our amazing kids.

Thanks to Michelle of Melissa Williams Design for the fabulous cover, and to our agent extraordinaire, Hannah Ekren, for her love and enthusiasm for these books. Thanks to Amy Carlin for being a proofreading goddess, and thanks to everyone who read and gave us notes throughout the many drafts of this project—especially Dantzel, Lauren, and Heather. Your feedback was invaluable and greatly appreciated.

And a special thanks to you, our readers. We hope you love these characters as much as we do.

Janci Patterson got her start writing contemporary and science fiction young adult novels, and couldn't be happier to now be writing adult romance. She has an MA in creative writing, and lives in Utah with her husband and two adorable kids. When she's not writing she can be found surrounded by dolls, games, and her border collie. She has written collaborative novels with several partners, and is honored to be working on this series with Megan.

Megan Walker lives in Utah with her husband, two kids, and two dogs—all of whom are incredibly supportive of the time she spends writing about romance and crazy Hollywood hijinks. She loves making Barbie dioramas and reading trashy gossip magazines (and, okay, lots of other books and magazines, as well.) She's so excited to be collaborating on this series with Janci. Megan has also written several published fantasy and science-fiction stories under the name Megan Grey.

Find Megan and Janci at www.extraseriesbooks.com

Other Books in the Extra Series

The Extra
The Girlfriend Stage
Everything We Are
The Jenna Rollins Real Love Tour
Starving with the Stars
My Faire Lady
You are the Story
Beauty and the Bassist
Su-Lin's Super-Awesome Casual Dating Plan
Exes, Lies, and Videotape

Made in the USA
Monee, IL
26 September 2019